Rolf Nagel

The End of the World Mafia

Publisher's imprint

Rolf Nagel

1st Edition 2016
© Rolf Nagel

Editor:
Dr. Anne Diefenbach

Translater
Ettie Kiene

Publisher
Tredition GmbH, Hamburg

978-3-7323-8102-9 (Paperback)
978-3-7323-8103-6 (Hardcover)
978-3-7323-8104-3 (eBook)

Content

Foreword

This novel describes the end of the international Mafia in 2020 and the story of a middle-class bank employee who - due to an intrigue - became the right-hand man of the Sicilian Mafia's supreme boss.

The author worked several decades as top manager in the international world of finance. As CEO of one of the first German risk capital firms that spoke out in favor of companies in the software world, he later gained deep insight into the financial flow of globally active equity investment banks.

It was inevitable and almost compulsory that he met dubious characters during such transactions. It must be said though that it is highly advisable not to get entangled personally in this shadow world.

For several years, the author developed the idea of writing a detective novel about the organization of the international Mafia. Own economic experiences were to contribute to the story. The novel does not lay any claim to scientific research and accuracy, but should reflect the author's personal impression.

During his own study of books, the author often experienced that he was unable to read a story from start to finish due to lack of time. Each time he started again, he had to re-read several sections in order to be able to follow the story. This novel serves to counteract this problem and represents light reading making it easier to get back into the story again due to its coherent chapters and paragraphs. Therefore, it is well suited for vacation time or travels.

The author wishes to let economic circumstances slip into the story without demanding economic knowledge from the reader. Although there is by no lack of drama, it is not just another of the numerous bloodthirsty Mafia stories available.

The novel gives an account of the daily life of the person pulling the strings and provides a glimpse into his future. Mafia players in today's business world operate much less conspicuously than is generally assumed.

It cannot be ruled out that some events have actually occurred as described or will develop like this in the future. However, all actions are purely fictional. Similarities with places, activities or people are purely coincidental.

I hope you enjoy it.

The banker became victim of a sweet intrigue

Karl Grosser was torn out of his bourgeois existence and advanced to international Mafia boss through an intrigue. He was a tall, handsome man with strong distinctive cheekbones and a high sex appeal. He always laid emphasis on appropriate clothing and lived a well-balanced life. Had his life not been turned upside down in one single weekend, there would actually have been nothing special to report about him.

Like every Sunday, he walked alone along the promenade reflecting on his past life. He was satisfied with himself even though many of his colleagues considered him a bore. At 40, he had made it to a nice condominium and had been employed for many years as head of organization of a private financial institution. What more did he want? Women did not play any major role in his life and in his opinion that was a good thing. After all, didn't he see enough failed marriages and disastrous love affairs that regularly resulted in chaos?

In order to enjoy the sunset during his walks, he always sat at the river bank on a park bench that he already considered as his own. On this particular day, he also approached "his" park bench that he could see already from a distance of about 300 meters.

However, what was that? This had never happened in all the years. Somebody was sitting on his bench! It looked like a conspiracy, an attack on his person.

As he approached, he noticed the curves of an elegant woman. However, he did not intend to approach this person. This was maybe a woman who he would fall in love with without this being reciprocated. He could not expose himself to such a danger. What should he do? He wondered how he could deal with this surprise. Should he pass by without a glance and forego the delights of the sunset? Alternatively, should he maybe sit down on the park bench beside her? Fully ignoring her concentrated femininity of course.

When he was only a few meters from the park bench, he was forced to make a quick decision. To his own surprise, he addressed the pretty woman saying, "Hallo, may I sit here?"

At that precise moment, he had no idea what that small question would mean for the future of mankind. Cheerfully and with a smile on her red lips, the perky person answered, "With pleasure, sir."

With a short "thank you" he sat down next to her turning slightly away from her just to be on the safe side. He had been courteous enough in his opinion. He had no intention of continuing the conversation in any way at all. His growing anger also let little room for it, even though she was very pretty.

They sat several centimeters away from each other on his park bench, legs crossed in the same direction, something every psychology student would probably have interpreted as being a mutual expression of interest. Some time passed by without any communication between the two. Had this woman not launched the next attack, the story could already have ended here.

The young woman opened her outrageously expensive handbag and pulled out a gold cigarette case from which she took a lady's cigarette. Then she continued rummaging around in her bag as if she was searching through a suitcase large enough for a journey lasting several weeks. Karl played his part as if he hadn't noticed what was going on.

After a while, he heard her say, "Excuse me, sir, do you have a light?" Karl could hardly believe his ears. However, as he was a gentleman, he couldn't just ignore the question. Yes, he did have a lighter in his pocket. As a non-smoker, he only had it with him for occasions such as these. The elegant piece was not used often, but it had a right to exist for just such situations.

Without taking a closer look at the feminine curves, he opened his jacket and pulled out a shiny lighter from his inside pocket. He loved this ritual and sometimes wished he were a smoker simply to be able to enjoy this masculine role more often. With an elegant flip of the hand, he opened the lighter cap igniting the flame with practiced fingers.

The young lady drew closer to the flame puffing clumsily in order to light the cigarette. Even before the cigarette began to glow, the pleasant, sweet fragrance of her perfume reached Karl's nostrils. He couldn't help but take note of well-rounded female proportions in her discreet cleavage. He noted how his body flew into unwanted surges of emotion. He felt a mixture of anger and unsuspected longing. His feelings were similar to those of a gladiator in the arena.

Wallowing in a haze of feelings, he heard the provocative voice of his neighbor once again, "Thank you, my name is Marian." He answered automatically, "Karl, my name is Karl Grosser." "Karl, were you born here?", he heard her ask in almost perfect German. The accent though implied a Romanic native language such as Spanish or Italian. Balancing between intimacy and respect, Marian chose well by using the combination of the formal "you" and first name which is unusual in Germany.

"Yes, I have spent my whole life in this city." He looked into her beautiful black eyes and noticed her subtly made-up facial features.

Immediately she added, "This really is a beautiful small town with a very special charm. It is probably even more beautiful to experience the city in togetherness. Unfortunately, I am here on my own today."

Karl wondered what she meant with this foolish talk of togetherness. He doubted that this direct manner corresponded with her natural upbringing. She couldn't be one of those women professionally committed to prostitution, could she? Nevertheless he replied politely, "I could imagine a beautiful woman like you has a partner at her side." "That is unfortunately not the case, but that may change. What about you, Karl? ", he heard her say. Karl replied, "My work leaves me little time for that, that hasn't happened yet."

He rejected the idea that Marian could be a prostitute. Impossible that that kind of woman could display such education and appearance. This was probably a lady from high society.

They chatted for a while about the city and its attractions when he suddenly heard, "Karl, I would be very happy if you would be my guest for dinner this evening and keep me company. Perhaps you can tell me more about your city? I hope you don't mind me asking."

Beguiled and completely unprepared for this offer, Karl replied with a simple "Yes, with pleasure!" After he uttered these words he was surprised at himself and realized that he had unexpectedly agreed to a rendezvous.

A sudden loud crash rang out and Karl turned around, startled. Also totally horrified, his neighbor looked behind her. There they saw that two cars had collided. Marian's face was now even paler than before. In that moment of shock it had not been possible to distinguish that the loud bang had come from the crash. It sounded rather like an exploding bomb. The resulting shock was greater than the situation was actually worth. Nothing had happened to the passengers. They got out of their vehicles safely and unharmed discussing loudly who the party at fault was. Nevertheless, Marian had gotten such a fright that she became a bit hectic.

Marian turned back to Karl and said, "Fine, please allow my chauffeur to pick you up at eight o'clock. Is that okay for you, Karl?"

She looked at him unrelentingly with a questioning glance. Again, he retorted automatically, "Yes! Yes, of course, with pleasure!"

Still thinking that stuttering was not really his thing, Karl pulled a private business card out of his jacket and handed it to her without saying a word.

"I am really pleased, Karl, so we will meet for dinner. Unfortunately, I have to go now." She stood up and walked towards the parking lot. This strength-sapping effort was indeed a bit too much for the inexperienced Marian. She was happy to have dealt with the matter so well.

From a distance, Karl saw her getting into a white limousine with a man holding the rear door open. Afterwards, the man got in the chauffeur's seat and started up the engine.

A huge jolt ran through Karl's body. What had just happened? He had just been torn out of his unchanging life by a few sentences. In just a few minutes, his evening had been planned without him having had the opportunity to oppose it. It was as if he was in a trance. He had not experienced anything like it in his entire life.

Should he be pleased? Or worried? Without his cooperation, someone had crept into his life. Moreover, someone from the female species, and he had not even able to use his male hunting instincts. Somewhat flattered he accepted his fate. His inexperience with the opposite sex was clearly to be blamed for the way his life had suddenly changed. What consequences would this have for his future life? It was all just terrible. However, there was no way he would give the date a miss.

He had to compose himself and develop a plan of action. Looking at his new, luxury watch, he noticed that he had only two hours left.

That was much too short a time to develop a plan with appropriate countermeasures. And he couldn't call any of his few friends. They would never have believed his story, even though he was regarded as being absolutely worthy of belief. Therefore, he set off quickly in the direction of his apartment.

On the first floor he unlocked his door and entered the apartment quickly. After closing the door he was in his most familiar surroundings. Here he felt safe and secure once again. Security - that was his life motto. However, in what unforeseeable adventure had he got himself into?

Shower and shave, do your hair and find a shirt, tie and a matching suit in a hurry. Pure stress! The phone rang and he raced out of the bathroom to answer the call. "Mother, I am very sorry, I have no time. No, mother, everything is fine! Yeah, sure. Yes, definitely. It's only I have a date with a lady. What? No, no, no wedding. What put that idea into your head? You will definitely get her to know first, if necessary! I will tell you tomorrow. See you then."

Dear God, his mother was already thinking about marriage. But that wasn't something he could think about now.

He talked to himself, "I'm in a hurry! The clock is ticking!" What can a man do in the remaining hour? Ah! Socks, but where are they? Yes, of course, in the closet! One? But there are always two! A breast pocket handkerchief to match the suit and a matching tie. The sock! Where is that damn sock? One black and one gray.

This is not something that usually happens to him. He normally always has everything in order. Everything had its place. But what now? Today of all days everything was chaotic. Now the entire apartment seemed to be the epitome of disorder. Shoes! Yes, there! Wonderful. Put them on. There are two of the same, therefore one pair. The best thing is a pair. Stop! First the socks. But still two different ones. Only a cognac could help here. He called himself to order, "Karl, cognac in the afternoon? No, that will not do, that will never do!" So he put the bottle back.

Karl thought, "I am never going to manage like this. I have to start things systematically - as always. First the underwear, then the socks, then the shirt and finally knot the tie."

There were still a whole 30 minutes left. It was an apparently impossible task in this short time. The second sock and it's exactly the same color, two matching shoes, a pair. Wonderful!

Karl was actually ready to take part in the Olympics. Now go to the mirror! He knotted his tie skillfully around his neck, in the collar intended for it. Perfect! Next! Pants! A man needs a belt for his pants. Jacket. Ready!

Awesome! Everything in a record time of just 50 minutes. His inner voice reminded him just in time about flowers. What? That too? Yes, flowers. But first the cufflinks. Where do you get flowers? But a gentleman has to have flowers, at least for a first date. It was clear to him already that from now on everything in his life would be chaos.

Nevertheless, he still had to go to work as usual the next day. The best thing would be for him to go to a doctor tomorrow to get a sick note. He could not possibly work in the condition he is in at the moment. Until now, he hadn't been absent one single hour during his entire working life.

Only 15 minutes left. His world was close to ruins. Only a tsunami could bring him salvation. But this would probably not happen in Germany before 8 o'clock. No use moaning about it.

He rushed down the stairs. A florist - his rescue! It was as if everyone was rushing to get flowers. He had never seen anything like it. At the same time, he realized that he had probably not entered a flower shop during the last 20 years. Mother always got chocolates, the ones with the liquid centers. He finally made it to the head of the queue. The florist put together the most beautiful bouquet of flowers he had ever seen. He had the feeling that it cost more than the overall costs for the German reunification. Oh dear, he had to pay! His wallet was at home. He had never seen the shop clerk before in his life, yet she said, "No problem. Pay tomorrow, I know you. "

He raced back to his apartment. Everything was going well, nothing could go wrong anymore. His apartment door bell rang. He jumped to the window. He saw a white limousine on the road, a Rolls Royce. "This is my car for tonight? Middle-class Karl in a Rolls Royce?", he thought skeptically and hoped no-one from the neighborhood would see him entering the swanky limousine. If that happened, they would think he had won in the lottery.

He crept quietly down the stairs, opening and closing the front door without making a noise.

"Mr. Karl Grosser?", he heard the chauffeur in a gray suit ask. At the same time, the chauffeur opened the rear door of the car. Karl looked around to see if anyone in the neighborhood had heard anything and got into the car quickly.

White leather seats. The vehicle doors closed with the same sound as the armored safe doors in his bank. Was this soft humming the road noise of the limo? A prince could not be rushed through the streets better. Expensive cars like this were not common in Karl's city. It was just as well that the car windows reflected so that nobody could see him. It would be unthinkable if his colleagues saw him in this limo. The bank would probably drag him in front of the anti-corruption committee and suspend him.

If only, as an exception, he hadn't gone for a walk that terrible day, or at least scurried past the park bench. Then he would have been spared all this fuss. Nevertheless, he wanted to meet the requirements of his new position in society.

Marian had been sitting in the private room of the restaurant for quite a while already thinking about the encounter with Karl that she and her father had been planning meticulously for several weeks. She actually already knew more about Karl than anybody else in his life.

The Mafia boss worried about his daughter's future

Together with her father, the daughter had found out about all of Karl's habits. What shoes he wore on which days, what food he preferred etc. Marion even knew about Karl's prostitute who he kept very secret and who he visited now and again. Despite this, she had to play her continued role of ignorance. Only by doing this was the success of the activity planned for the coming weeks ensured.

With Marian's 24th birthday laying ahead, her father Don Serjo Rosso began to think about a future husband for his daughter. The provocative Marian had been receiving numerous advances from quite attractive men since her early youth, however except for a few brief and insignificant affairs these remained unsuccessful.

Don Serjo Rosso, the boss ("capo di tutti capi") of the international Mafia, was known to the public only as a serious and impeccable businessman. Don was not the right term for a boss, more the term "capo". He was given the nickname Don, which was actually only entitled for heads of churches, at an early stage. He liked it and that's the way it stayed.

The Don had never come to the attention of the legal system. There were no vague speculations anywhere in the world that he ruled over a global Mafia network. In addition to his Mafia organization, Don Rosso had a vast network of interlaced company investments at his disposal. As head of the criminal organization – of the so-called honorable family - he remained unchallenged at the top of the hierarchical structure. The subordinate bosses formed the three ranks, ranks 1-3, behind him.

Just like the members of the first rank, the Don had inherited his position from his father. It was only possible to be included in the organization's first rank and inner circle through inheritance. If someone died without a male heir, the seat was closed and the tasks were distributed to the others. This security measure ensured that possible betrayers in the inner circle could be ruled out permanently. This had already been the top priority of the forefathers. Don Rosso was only personally known to the members of the inner circle, and he made sure that it stayed like this.

The information exchange in the inner circle took place via so-called messengers. This procedure had been found to be extremely efficient and safe over decades and generations.

Don Rosso had a top-secret plan to reorganize the entire structure of the Mafia by 2020. Nothing should remain the way it was. He had entrusted this long-term project to no-one, not even to his closest confidants and planned a period of seven years for its implementation.

Even though he was already approaching his seventies, Don Rosso was still both physically and mentally fit. With intelligence and foresight, he wanted to take measures relevant for the future of his family members. Although the family members had always kept up to date with the latest technology, it was time to reposition the entire organization.

Don Rosso was a highly educated and intelligent man and he was aware of the fact that only a long-term and sensitive approach would help deal with such an enormous task successfully. No mistakes were allowed. The entire organization was at stake. If the project failed, everything could be wiped out at one time. In addition, he needed an absolutely trustworthy person to implement his plan. It had to be ensured that not a single word would escape the chosen person's lips.

Also important to him was that the person was able to cope with such a daunting task with great spirit and organizational skills. There was nobody suitable for this purpose in the inner circle. Therefore, an outsider had to be found. But this was no easy feat. In whose mind could Don Rosso look with absolute certainty? Mistakes could destroy the families and drive them to ruin forever. He had also not developed any ideas on how to let his closest confidants in on this project. Would they not support the plan for reasons of risk or maybe even reject the restructuring?

Marian's father developed a plan to find a husband for Marian who at the same time would be the co-designer of the reorganization. If his daughter's future spouse could also perform the tasks of the realignment, this would be an excellent solution to some of the problems. Of course, Don Rosso had not mentioned all this to his daughter.

Her father's proposal to work together to find her a spouse didn't appeal to Marian in the least, but with the powers of persuasion, her father was able to convince his daughter to try this idea out. Her father countered Marian's desire to find a suitable life partner by herself with the argument that his action could only strengthen her efforts. After a while he was able to convince his daughter so far that she was at least willing to try it out.

Using a contact man, Don Rosso dispatched scouts all over the world with the task of finding a suitable husband in accordance with his and Marian's predefined criteria. Apart from the usual requirements, it was also important that the man was intelligent and well-versed in the financial world. In addition, he should have great organizational skills, be totally inconspicuous to the police and extremely reliable.

Father and daughter had looked at countless dossiers and photographs taken by the scouts. Potential candidates weren't supposed to notice anything about what was going on. Finally, there only a few men shortlisted by Marian and Don Rosso. What remained were an Italian, an American and Karl from Germany. These three candidates were cased again more closely in order to lay out their life stories clearly on the table. Recorded videos of the three gave father and daughter an even better picture and replaced a personal inspection.

The intriguer's decision was made

Marian and her father decided in favor of Karl. Yes, without noticing what had been happening, Karl was selected as the chosen one. He was the chosen one for the grand overall project.

Although Marian was still a bit queasy at the thought, father and daughter developed a plan for a first meeting between her and Karl. The victim's regular walks were most suitable and harmless for this purpose. Only the park bench of course came into question as a place of approach.

Should in spite of the dossier and the video shooting the daughter find no liking for Karl during a live encounter, she could withdraw from the situation at any time. The candidate would never know that he had been on the shortlist and about the plan that the father and daughter had come up with.

The meeting on the park bench and the invitation to dinner completed the first steps successfully. Marian had definitely taken a liking to Karl. Moreover, despite her concerns and her bad conscience, she felt attracted to Karl.

As she waited for him in the hotel restaurant she began to have doubts again. Will this daring endeavor really be a success? Should she not tell Karl about it at a later point in time? Tell him that he had become the victim of an intrigue without noticing it? Even worse - that she was main perpetrator in this plan.

So as not to face these unpleasant issues any longer, Marian decided not to give further thought to the matter for the time being. There was not much time for that anyway because, as the chauffeur had informed her by phone, Karl was already in the car on his way to her.

Karl took great pleasure in letting himself be chauffeured through his city. Not having to drive himself was something new for him. He saw things he never experienced when he drove himself. The chauffeur drove him in a quiet and dignified way through the streets of the city arriving at the gates of the excellent hotel just five minutes before the agreed time.

The hotel of course had several stars and other awards and was the temporary luxury home of royalty. A page standing at the entrance dressed in livery and a black top hat opened the car door. Karl's chauffeur informed him subtly that Karl was a guest of Madame Rosso. He led Karl in a dignified way into the overwhelmingly large lobby where the concierge at the reception desk greeted him with the words, "Madame Rosso is awaiting you, Mr. Grosser, allow me to show you the way."

This meaningless chatter of the hotel staff was nothing new to Karl. Having attended some bank events, he knew how to behave and move around in such situations.

You had to react to the hotel employee's pompous speech that is a remnant of the last century in an assured and sensitive way. These people recognize immediately whether you measure up to the situation or not.

The consequence of carelessness is that when you are arrogant, you end up being ostracized by the whole hotel. All the more because, from the staff's point of view, generous tips are not to be expected. In these noble hotels, it is the hotel staff's compulsory way of thinking that the holy halls should only be entered by the appropriate clientele. Getting out of the ostracism of the hotel staff is usually as an impossible task.

The hotel concierge moved elegantly through the hotel lobby and led Karl through the restaurant area towards a door marked "Private". When he opened the door, Karl entered a dining room that had the elegance of the '20s. Numerous silver candlesticks with lighted white candles, costly carpets, a great English fireplace and a dining table with seating for twelve gave the room that dignified something. It reminded you of a journey from the past century through to modern times. We are after all living in the year 2013 with internet and 3-D televisions.

Marian sat at the end of the long table and the concierge announced Karl's arrival, "Madame, Mr. Grosser." Karl handed Marian the bouquet of flowers and a waiter appeared straight away carrying a large vase made of crystal glass.

At the same time, Karl noticed a man in a black suit standing at the back of the room. According to his stature and behavior, he could easily recognize him as being a bodyguard. My God, what kind of a theatrical performance will this evening be for Karl?

The conclusion of an already messed up Sunday?

"Please sit down, Karl." Again, he noticed Marian's use of this strange combination of the formal "you" and "first name". Nevertheless, Karl obeyed without questioning. Before him stood a battery of different wine glasses. The amount of cutlery led to the conclusion that they would probably not just be having a snack. A 6-course menu at least was to be expected. He remembered that cutlery is used from the outside to the inside for the individual courses of a dinner. He could cope with the etiquette of upper society at least to this extent.

"Did you have a pleasant afternoon?", Marian asked. His answer came quickly, "A charming afternoon." He didn't tell her that the stress had almost brought him to the brink of collapse.

One of the elegantly dressed waiters brought them a sherry as an aperitif. He staged this scene solemnly. Then Marian turned to Karl, "I would like to know more about you. What do you do as a profession? "

He said, "I have been working in an international private bank as head of organization for many years now. The Image Bank AG has its headquarters in the city."

"Oh, what a coincidence, my father is also a good customer of that bank and has his business accounts there. The manager and he are long-standing friends."

Marian play acted skillfully, as if she were amazed at the coincidence. In fact, she, of course, already knew this from the dossier.

The two of them spent a very harmonious evening together. They enjoyed each course of the menu, even though the food was so clearly arranged on the plate that you actually needed a plan to find it.

During their amusing conversation, they found out that they have quite a lot in common. Marian was amused by Karl's life story and they both became increasingly closer. This very pretty and elegant woman had found interest in Karl's person. He had never dreamed before that this could be possible. She could with certainty bewitch every man with her charming smile and well-shaped body. What did this woman see in the rather inconspicuous and unobtrusive Karl?

Just before 9.30 p.m. Marian said, "Karl, shall we have our espresso in my suite?"
He immediately replied, "That is an excellent idea."

She stood up and walked to a door at the end of the room, Karl followed her nervously. Behind the wooden door was a lift which led directly to the top floor of the hotel. After leaving the elevator, the bodyguard entered the floor with the sign "Presidential Suite" first, followed by Marian and Karl. The front door of the suite was opened by the bodyguard, but he himself did not enter. After Karl and Marian had entered the room, the bodyguard closed the door from the outside again.

"Truly beautiful and elegant", Karl said. He left the question open whether he meant the suite, Marian or both.

They sat down on the sofa in the living room, a butler entered from an adjoining room and served espresso. Karl was telling his companion some stories about his city when Marian took the plunge and put her arms around Karl. She kissed him deeply and Karl returned the embrace. At this precise moment, they both realized that their evening together was far from its end.

When Karl woke up the next morning, daylight was trying to squeeze through the thick brocade curtains. Just enough daylight so that he could look at his clock. Was it all a dream? He looked around and watched Marian ecstatically. She was still in a deep sleep, this beautiful and charming woman. He pinched his arm to make sure that this was all not just a beautiful dream.

Then he looked at the clock and was shocked, it was 10.23 a.m. "Hell!" he yelled. "I have to go to the bank, for heaven's sake." In all the years he had never been late for work. What would Mr. Schneider, his superior, say? Exaggerated thoughts immediately rushed through Karl's head. Maybe he would get a written warning or maybe even his notice?

Meanwhile, slowly and gently, Marian was wakening from her sleep. She looked at Karl questioningly, "Karl, what is wrong?"

"I have to go to the bank straight away, I'm late", he

shouted excitedly whirling his shirt around clumsily.

The boss used his contacts in favor of the banker

Marian kept calm and said, "Oh Karl, I completely forgot. Yesterday I called my father and asked him to phone the executive director of your bank and ask for two days off so that we can get to know each other better. That wasn't a problem because my father - as I said before - has been friends with the director for many years."

Karl looked at Marian in surprise. "What? How? Your father has discussed me with the director of the bank?" Karl Grosser, a small department head, had never even exchanged a single word with the director. It was quite inconceivable that the director even knew he existed.

His breath caught at the thought that the director himself was approving his vacation. Who was he? He who only knew his next boss, Vice President Schneider, personally? It was nowhere possible that he would have the opportunity of entering the holy corridors of the executive director. Nevertheless, he slowly liked the idea that the executive director was learning about the existence of Karl Grosser.

His thoughts however quickly went in the direction of possible sources of danger. What would happen if he and Marian ever had differences? Which concentrated power would come down on him then? And would he, little Karl, even survive? Two hearts beat in his chest now. It was undoubtedly clear to him that Marian was telling the truth. Her father actually had these contacts, the situation was by no means doubtful, or was it maybe a bit?

"Let's have a quiet breakfast and then you can stop by the bank. Maybe we can take a stroll through the city beforehand? In the afternoon, I am flying to Paris to meet my father, but I will be back in the evening. Karl, I would love to have dinner again with you this evening. The car and chauffeur are of course at your disposal for as long as you like.", Marian said, in an almost determined voice.

There was no doubt about it. She had fallen head over heels in love with Karl. Although this was something that she had always only ever hoped for, this happy state of affairs had actually happened. Karl also felt the same butterflies in his stomach.

"Good, then I will do my work in the bank and we will meet at the same time, at 8.00 p.m.," Karl said, acting as if this was all natural for him. But it wasn't. Within only a few hours, his peaceful and always un-changed life was turned completely upside down. Each minute brought a new surprise. He was just about to ask himself again whether he would survive it all without harm. Or should he maybe go and see a doctor as a precaution?

The magnificent hotel breakfast left nothing to be de-sired. Afterwards, they strolled together through the city center. Karl saw his city with new eyes - never be-fore had he actually registered these outrageously ex-pensive luxury stores. He frequently went past them, but the fact that the prices did not fit with his wallet always caused him to scurry past the shop windows.

Marian enjoyed devoting herself to the beautiful things of life together with her new companion. She was also unconcerned about the price. She was used to this life of luxury and for her this was something natural. The expedition through the city was very harmonious for both of them.

The lovers drove to the airport and Karl said goodbye giving her an intimate kiss before she boarded the private MacDonnell Douglas MD 83 plane. Marian could, of course, hardly wait to tell her father everything in detail and was looking forward to seeing him in Paris.

Karl let himself be driven to the bank by limousine. The car arrived at the grand and impressive main entrance of the bank. The glass building radiated a modern character. He got out of the limousine, his legs shaking. Wondering what would expect him next, he climbed the steps to the entrance hall of the bank and greeted the doorman. He called out, "Hallo, Mr. Grosser, have a good day." On other days, only an unintelligible murmur escaped his mouth. Karl went to the elevator and waited. The doors opened and, as usual, he rode up to the last but one floor. At least he had got up this far, the only floor above his was the executive floor. The elevator doors had hardly opened when one of his colleagues walked past him. This was one of those colleagues who was permanently full of intrigues. "Hello Mr. Grosser, I hope you had a nice day."

Karl was angry. So he also already knew that he had not been in the bank this morning. He walked across the hall area and got to his office where his assistant welcomed him over-friendly and visibly excited, "Mr. Grosser, Mr. Schneider already informed me that you have new tasks and will not be expected at work today or tomorrow."

Karl's thoughts tumbled, "New tasks? Are they going to fire me or am I maybe going to be transferred to the record office? Surely Marian hasn't lied to me and her father didn't arrange holiday for me after all!" His stomach slowly started turning and he started to feel ill. He had to clarify this straight away and he rushed out of his office across the hallway into Mr. Schneider's outer office.

His assistant gave Karl a very warm welcome and congratulated him. Karl thought she wanted to make fun of him and wished the ground would swallow him up.

"Mr. Grosser, I've been asked to show you in as soon as you arrive", she said. "Perfect! That's a fine mess I'm in, instant dismissal.", is what went through his head as he entered Mr. Schneider's office. "Ah, Mr. Grosser, what a surprise, you are back already? We didn't expect you before tomorrow or the day after. Please take a seat. Would you like coffee or tea?" Karl was in despair. His slimy boss, that stinker, was making fun of his humiliating dismissal. But it was too late now, he had to endure it.

"I was a bit surprised when the director informed me

personally that you, my dear Mr. Grosser, are now personally responsible for taking care of a major client of the bank. He informed me that you are freed immediately from all other duties and are no longer subject to any working time control.

In addition, your salary has been doubled by the management board and a generous entertainment budget has been set up for you. You must have landed a big contract. Who would have thought it!" As he spoke, Mr. Schneider raised his eyebrows at the same time looking quite astonished.

Karl couldn't believe his ears at what he was hearing. So he wasn't being dismissed, he was being promoted! He was in seventh heaven! He could hardly believe his ears, however he wanted to play his new role confidently so that not the slightest doubt could arise. Double the salary, an entertainment budget, exemption from working and attendance times. All that was now Mr. Karl Grosser - a former small head of organization who almost had to kneel down to Mr. Schneider when he wanted to buy a new chair.

He had now become the personal advisor of a major client even though there were noticeably better specialized advisors in the bank and he was actually head of organization and not an advisor. What a rapid rise!

"Then I should get down to work straight away for my client!" said Karl taking polite but firm leave of Mr. Schneider and started to leave the office. "Of course, Mr. Grosser, and if you need anything please call me anytime," Mr. Schneider called as he was leaving. Karl felt intoxicated by what he was hearing. He went down the hall to his office. His assistant was waiting for him saying, "Mr. Grosser, good that you are here! Ms. Rosso is on the line. Should I put her through to your office?" Karl answered while passing by, "Yes, and tea please." "Right away, Mr. Grosser!"

Karl took the receiver of his phone and heard Marian's voice, "Hello my love, I've landed already. How are you? I miss you already." "Everything is great, I can hardly describe it, it's all such a whirl. I just got a raise and I have been released from my normal duties to act as your advisor. Of course, day and night, my love. Marian, I am floating on cloud nine. Best wishes and many thanks to your father even though we have not yet met. I hope to meet him in person soon. Kisses." Karl was totally exuberant.

"I love you too, my dear. It was a beautiful evening and a great night. I wouldn't have wanted to miss a single second of it. I still have some time till I meet my father and I would like to buy you a small gift. Yes, I will give your regards to my father. See you later and take care of yourself. Kisses!" Karl drank his tea with pleasure recalling the scene in peace. Then he left the bank and approached the chauffeur in the parking lot. "Drive me back to my apartment, please. I would like to change my clothes."

The apartment door closed and Karl sank down on his bed with a deep sigh. Just five minutes rest, just a bit of rest. Some time passed, then he went into the bathroom to finally take a shower and shave. Then he slipped into a new shirt and suit. Whistling, he went to the flower shop to pay his outstanding bill to surprise his beloved again with a colorful bouquet of flowers. "Ah, the gentleman from yesterday! Are you now visiting us every day?", the pretty florist greeted him. In his rush the previous day Karl hadn't noticed that she was a youthful beauty who, with her long black hair, was easily the center of attention. Karl replied, "I need a colorful bouquet, but one that is slightly larger than yesterday. No, make that double the size." "Of course, sir," said the florist and throwing back her magnificent head of hair in a skilful and sexy way.

He noticed that the young lady was flirting a bit with him. That never used to happen. Maybe love made sexy or it had something to do with fact that he used to be grumpy and rude to everyone. It didn't displease him that this young woman probably found him attractive. Karl was amazed at how quickly things can change. Yesterday he was still Calamity Jane and today Cinderella.

Marian had arrived in Paris a little earlier than planned and strolled along the famous Champs-Élysées, a magnificent avenue with every luxury store you could think of. The sun shone down warmly on the avenue and the people strolled along happily. Marian had in the meantime bought her darling Karl a fine gold chain with a heart pendant. Her destination was now the exclusive café and restaurant on the corner. There on nice days you could sit outside watching the colorful crowds. Just like her father, she loved to just sit there and let her mind wander. She had a lot of things in common with her father in other respects too.

Everybody enjoyed a first-class education in a Swiss residential school

Like her father, Marian had spent her youth in an outrageously expensive residential school in Switzerland.

The fathers of the first rank and Don Rosso's father had been extremely farsighted and had sent their children to this private residential school. Thus, the descendants could spend their youth together and receive an excellent education.

Another reason was that the children were able to establish a firm and trusting friendship and bond with this joint school time. This was also something the fathers wanted. The inner circle should enter a hard and fast trust association and what could be better than starting this when still at school. And this is also what Don Rosso did with his daughter.

The strict residential school was located on a small hill directly on the outskirts of the idyllic Swiss town of Lucerne on the Lake of Lucerne. From the hill, you could look down at the beautiful little town with its river and famous landmark chapel bridge.

In wintertime, you went to the mountains for skiing and in the summer you could swim in the lake. Apart from that, only the children of the wealthiest parents resided in the school, something that also helped the young people establish the best contacts in international and influential society. Nobody at the residential school of course knew about the true background that some of the parents had in the Mafia.

Marian remembered vaguely that there had only been one slip-up when a boy made a comment that there were children there who came from criminal families. This claim couldn't be proven and Don Rosso and his friends immediately complained to the school management. The boy then had to leave the school and nothing was ever heard of him or his family again. It was never clarified whether the boy's statement was based on mere supposition or if there were reasonable grounds for suspicion behind it.

The families' wives and children had never been involved in the affairs of the fathers. They only heard in passing that the fathers belonged to a secret organization. But it was forbidden to talk about it even in the slightest way and nobody ever made the mistake of doing. Even thinking in this direction was absolutely forbidden. Most of them will probably have banned this completely from their minds.

Marian reached the café at the corner and saw Don Rosso with his sunglasses on sitting comfortably in the sun at a table for four. Before him stood a bottle of water and an espresso. His two bodyguards had seated themselves at a table at behind him and were carefully observing the scene.

Don Rosso still loved his hometown Palermo but in the meantime he was traveling to so many countries that he had dropped the typical habits of a Sicilian. He dressed more like a banker from London and had their middle-class features. Otherwise, he was of a normal build and there was nothing particular eye-catching about his appearance. He had always been a very loving father who found the right balance between the necessary strictness and generous love in the education of his only daughter.

After the early death of her mother because of an incurable disease, Don Rosso took over also the maternal part and tried to fulfil this role as well as he could. Marian and her father treated each other in a trustful manner and had a strong bond. She only had the best memories of a happy childhood and her father always tried to fulfill every wish for her.

"Hi daddy," she said to him and kissed him on both cheeks. Her eyes spoke sweet volumes and Don Rosso was actually able to read everything from them.

"It is good to see you so happy, my daughter," he said, with his distinctive voice, "Yes, I can see everything in your face, but sit down and tell me all the details."

Marian told him of the encounter with Karl on the park bench. Everything went as planned and in addition, she had fallen head over heels in love with Karl without knowing why. She described everything enthusiastically and in such detail that Don Rosso felt as if he had been there himself.

As father he was now happy and pleased, especially because the hard work had borne fruit. Now it had to be ensured that Karl became a future player in the organization and everything would be perfect. Things could not have gone better for Don Rosso.

"Daddy, thank you so much that you interceded at the bank so quickly on Karl's behalf. He was clearly worried this morning about getting to the bank too late" She looked at her father gratefully and they both smiled about Karl's flustered state.

"Of course, my child, that was not a big deal for me and I of course want to see my princess happy. Enjoy a few weeks of vacation with him and then introduce me to the man who wants to take away my daughter."

With a friendly grin, he asked his daughter what she would like to order.

"Daddy, we should have some good champagne and drink to that." Don Rosso, who rarely drank alcohol, agreed to this and motioned to one of his guards who was dressed in black. The guard stood up straight away and walked over to a waiter to place the order.
"Where's your bodyguard?" Don Rosso asked his daughter.

"Oh daddy!" Marian dragged the two words out like chewing gum. "You always worry about me so lovingly, but there is no reason to do so. Karl accompanied me together with the chauffeur to the airport, well, and here ..."

She was interrupted by the approaching waiter who skillfully opened the champagne bottle with a pop and filled the glasses.

"My dear child, you know that these precautions are

perfectly appropriate and your Karl is not a trained security guard. Robbery and kidnapping always a topic. You read about it every day in the newspapers. So, please! For the future! Even if Karl is with you, I still want the security guard to be close by. This must be evident even to Karl." Don Rosso looked a bit grim now.

Neither he nor his daughter had ever been attacked, but in his eyes, the new Russian and Chinese clans were at least as unpredictable as the Sicilian Mafia had been in the early '20s.

"Okay, Daddy, I promise it will never happen again. Are you happy again now?" Marian looked at her father pleadingly like a small, sweet girl.

"Yes, my little one. Of course I am pleased and I suggest that you introduce the guy to me personally after your wonderful vacation."

"But Daddy the guy, his name is Karl! Please don't call him a guy. But are you sure you only want to meet him personally in a few week's time? You know, I am very certain about him!"

Don Rosso looked at his daughter a little surprised and replied, "It's not yet time to introduce Karl to me, and besides, I have urgent business in South America. Therefore we'll do that in a few week's time!"

Marian had learned never to question her father's words. Whenever he permitted no further responses to his comments, protest was pointless and would certainly not lead to success.

Like an old married couple they sat together for a while discussing everything possible until the sun set and it became a bit cooler. Don Rosso had his car drive up and brought his daughter to the airport.

As Marian and Karl sat together in the hotel restaurant at 8 o'clock that evening he told her of his experiences in the bank.

Marian said gushingly, "My dearest, let us spend a couple of weeks in Palermo, the city of my childhood, I would love to show you the sights. We could stay in our family home and go on excursions on the island. Oh my darling, that would be wonderful."

At the same time, as a so-called blackmail, Marian gave her lover the little gold chain that she had bought for him earlier in the day in Paris, and said casually, "Your bank has released you from your duties. And in a few week's time you will get to know my father personally. He is eager to talk to you. Father still has to do some urgent business meetings and will also be coming to Palermo afterwards." She was all smiles and nobody, especially not Karl, could have refused this request. So it was settled.

After Karl had packed his bags, they flew to Palermo the next day.

The lovers moved into the villa in Palermo

Karl and Marian drove in a luxurious limousine towards an ornamental iron-barred gate. After the guards had opened the gates, the car drove up the driveway until they arrived at the magnificent entrance. The impressive overall picture of this stylish villa with its green shimmering roof made it look like a colonial house from Wilhelminian times.

A crowd of servants stood in front of the white entrance and Karl felt as if he had been transported 100 years back in time. Yes, time had been forgotten and had come to a standstill here. From the front entrance, facilities such as a pool and patio at the back were not visible. Tall palm trees graced a neatly kept park.

Marian was delighted to show her darling the estate and the countless rooms with their green-mirrored windows.

Then they visited the park, where blooming flowers unfolded in a blaze of color. The sweet scent of flora was beguiling; a very suitable setting for young lovers riding the waves of romance. The scent of flowers filled the whole area including all rooms of the villa day and night.

The whole complex was heavily guarded by armed employees 24 hours a day therefore it was undoubtedly one of the safest places on the planet. The camera systems were camouflaged in such an excellent way that they left no traces in nature.

Enchanted, the two lovers spent their first night together and had a hearty breakfast on the terrace the following morning. As they roamed together through the grounds later on, they romped about and laughed. Karl thought there could be nothing that could harm this happiness.

A while later they went to the pool. Karl took a huge leap into the pool. This was his way of showing his courageous virility and water splashed onto the edge of the pool leaving Marian standing there like a drowned rat.

"Oh wait, you are going to pay for that." Marian also let herself fall into the pool in order to duck the rascal's head under water. Karl wasn't to be recognized any more, he had found a completely new lease of life and enjoyed his male role willingly.

In the coming weeks, Karl got better acquainted with each corner of the villa and the grounds, but not the secret work area that was hidden behind a sealed and concealed door. He would be allowed to visit these personally at a later point in time.

The loving couple spent a wonderful time going on walks along the beach and visiting the most beautiful places in Palermo. They enjoyed the Sicilian cuisine, the dry red wine and the idyllic surroundings.
However, the happiness of love was overshadowed by a phone call from the university hospital.

One afternoon when Karl's mobile phone rang, he answered as usual, "Karl Grosser, good day." On the other end of the line a lady said, "University Hospital of Cologne, My name is Westfal. Mr. Grosser, are you the son of Mrs. Silvia Grosser?"

Concerned Karl replied, "Yes, that's my mother, what has happened?" He sat down on the chair that Marian had pulled towards him when she noticed by glancing at Karl that something serious was in the air.

"I'm very sorry, Mr. Grosser, your mother was admitted this afternoon with a weak heart." The woman's voice paused briefly. "Unfortunately, your mother died of heart failure two hours ago." Another pause. "I am very sorry, Mr. Grosser."

Shocked Karl sank down onto the chair, "How could that happen? Mother died? I'll come straight away!" He ended the conversation so that he could compose himself and Marian clasped the visibly shocked man in her arms to comfort him.

On the same day Karl and Marian flew to Cologne. Karl was very sorry that he had not introduced Marian to his mother beforehand. Now it was too late. She would have been so pleased that he had finally found the right woman.

Marian took care of her beloved touchingly and helped him organize the funeral.

The funeral was very small-scale. Two days after the funeral, they flew back to Palermo so that Karl could recover from his grief better and was not dwelling on memories.

It took a few days until the sorrowing man had recovered from his loss. Marian stood by his side constantly during that painful period and this deepened their feelings for each other even more. With Marian's help, Karl was gradually able to overcome his grief.

Several weeks passed by. One Monday, Karl said to his sweetheart, "I would like to go into the city on my own today, there is something I would like to buy. I am sure to be back in three or four hours."

Marian looked at him questioningly, but accepted the comment as there was no explanation forthcoming.

The staff at the villa and the chauffeur were all highly educated and spoke excellent English, therefore Karl had no communication problems with any of them. The chauffeur drove him to the city and he asked him to take him to a good jeweler.

The chauffeur stopped at a first-class jeweler and accompanied Karl into the shop. "I would like to purchase an elegant ring with diamonds for a young lady. However, it should be rather unique," Karl told the chauffeur who translated this into Italian for the goldsmith.

It had got around the city a long time ago already that Karl was living in the Villa Rosso and he was served everywhere kindly and politely. However, the jeweler did not have a ring that met his expectations. The same experience was repeated several times.

Just as Karl was about to give up, the maestro in the last shop showed him a particularly elegant and very unusual piece. The ring didn't appear a bit pretentious for a young lady and it was an exclusively crafted masterpiece with a diamond. It fully met his expectations.

Over the past few days, Karl had determined in his bliss to tackle his next adventure. Back at the Villa Rosso, he said nothing about his plans. When he saw Marian's questioning eyes he didn't want to torture her any longer and told her something totally harmless. What he said was, "I needed to think a bit about us and our future. And for that I simply needed some time. Alone! Do you understand? "

"I hope this means something good", she whispered. She wanted to change the subject quickly and suggested they go to the pool.

"No, I'd like to go down to the harbor with you and walk around there for a bit", Karl said. A short time later, the two of them were walking along the pier.

Karl had devised a particularly nice surprise for Marian for the evening and told the butler about his plan. He should prepare the pool, which was not visible from the villa, for a romantic dinner. The domestic staff took care of this task preparing the perfect setting for a unique and romantic experience.

The wedding bells rang but not without Don Rosso's consent

In the early evening, Karl took his beloved Marian by the hand and led her through the grounds to the pool. Two musicians with violins joined them. They began to play old love songs giving the evening a charming ambience.

The staff had prepared a dream made up of flowers and lanterns for popular Marian and her companion. The evening was a perfect setting for Karl's plans and could not be more romantic. After the meal, the musicians and staff all withdrew quietly.

Karl stood up, took Marian's hands gently and knelt down gracefully before her. Marian, surprised by all this, caught her breath for a second.

In a gentle voice he made his speech. "My love, you have shown me the stars in the sky. Within only a few weeks, you tore me out of my lethargic life and brought sunshine into my heart. My happiness is complete. I don't want to miss you for one second in my life. My darling girl, I want to ask you if you are willing to share your life with me for eternity. Are you, my beloved Marian, willing to be my wife?"

He pulled the ring out of his pocket and slipped it slowly and gently over her ring finger. She looked at Karl and the tears rolled down her cheeks. She was unable to say a sound for minutes. Her heart was pounding, she was happy that he had fulfilled her deepest dream.

She gave her lover a long kiss and then whispered in his ear, "Yes, of course. This is my deepest wish, my love, until the end of our days. You make me the happiest woman in the world. Karl, you mean everything to me."

Both were in seventh heaven. They embraced and caressed each other the whole evening. When it became a little cooler, Karl picked up his bride and carried her in his arms into the house, up into the bedroom. That night was the longest in the villa and would have no end.

At noon next day they both woke up bleary-eyed. Before going to breakfast, Marian of course wanted to share the news with her father by telephone. She dialed his mobile number.

"My dear child," said Don Rosso on the phone, "what's wrong so early in the morning?"

Marian's voice came thick and fast as she told him the good news. Don Rosso sat down and listened attentively to the happy stories.

"Well, that's great! How wonderful, fantastic, I wish you all the luck and all the best from the bottom of my heart!" Her father's heart beat faster and he was choked and touched. He could barely hold back his tears of joy. "I have two more days here. I can't come earlier. But pick me up at the airport please, then you can tell me about your happiness in more detail. I will finish my work quickly and earlier than planned and then I will come straight away. After all, I have to meet my future son."

After he had finished talking, he lingered on the chair for a few minutes more to gather his thoughts. He had not expected this happy news so quickly. He became a little nervous which was extremely rare for him.

After he had gathered himself a bit more, he felt great pleasure and laughed. Now it was only a question of whether he could integrate Karl into his organization in a clever way. He wanted to resolve this matter as quickly as possible. It was clear to him that he had to approach the matter in a careful and clever way. How would his newly acquired son-in-law react? A lot depended on Karl's reaction.

Two days later Marian picked her father up from the airport. She had gone there on purpose without her future husband so that she could speak to her father in private.

"Daddy, I am so happy, so indescribably happy. Karl and I want to get married very soon. Perhaps you will have a grandchild by next year. Oh, Daddy, everything is just wonderful." Marian was all smiles and her father was pleased to see her daughter so happy.
"Slow down, not so fast. We are not at a Formula 1 race, you have still time. Your dear mother and I didn't marry straight away either. You need to wait a while. You know the family rules! Karl has to officially ask for your hand in marriage. That is the tradition and we don't want to break it."

Now everything was going a bit too quickly for Don Rosso and as long as he had no clarity as to whether Karl would join the organization, he wanted to delay giving his consent a bit. But this, of course, he didn't want to reveal to his happy daughter.

Time was pressing now for Don Rosso, but he couldn't and didn't want to afford a hasty reaction. "Marian, as long as your sweetheart agrees to assist me in my business, I'm happy to see you marry him. After all, he is going to be part of the family soon. I think he can take care of our company interests. What do you think?" Marian agreed to this idea.

"But please, I want to discuss this in a private conversation with your future husband, so keep quiet about it." Don Rosso looked at his daughter sternly and there was no doubt that his comment was not meant seriously.

The next day, father, daughter and Karl sat in the park chatting. The future son-in-law had quickly gained the friendship of Don Rosso and they talked to each other like old friends already. They had respect for each other and Don Rosso felt encouraged that his project would be completed soon.

"Karl, I would like to have a chat with you alone. Would tomorrow be okay for you? In the meantime, Marian can go and do a bit of shopping in the city. I could imagine our conversation from man to man will continue into the evening." Don Rosso looked at Karl in a friendly and questioning manner.

"Of course, that's not a problem. What do you think Marian?" This was just a formal question and she agreed, nodding. She preferred to go shopping together with Karl, but she knew she had no right to be consulted when it came to business, just like her mother.

The next day Don Rosso was up very early and ran back and forth excitedly in the park. He wondered how he should start the conversation with Karl. First, he only wanted to involve him in the legitimate company investments as a controller. The question was whether he would automatically get insight into the network of the Mafia organization while doing this work. Therefore, should he maybe inform Karl about his true identity now already or should he wait?

He considered the pros and cons and played out all the possible reactions in his head. Outing himself without knowing how Karl would react could quickly backfire.
The engaged couple finally arrived on the terrace. They took breakfast together. Then Karl said goodbye to Marian kissing her deeply. "See you later, my love and leave a few things in the stores for the Sicilians", he said with a mischievous smile.

"Yes, all the best then, Daddy, all the best. Karl, I will be back in the evening." Marian disappeared in the direction of the parking lot.

"We have a conference room. Come on, let's go there, we have a lot to talk about." Don Rosso stood up and slowly walked into the house. In the living room, he opened an armored door which was hidden behind another door and could only be opened with an access code. Behind it, a work area with offices and conference rooms equipped with every comfort opened up in front of Karl.

"Our predecessors created this work area and held their meetings here. You know, there is nothing worse than being spied on. That's normal these days.", Don Rosso informed his future son-in-law and led the way through several rooms until he came to a room that was a bit cooler. The room looked odd and a bit depressing, more like a large prison cell.

"Very depressing", Karl said, looking a bit concerned. "This room is like a Faraday cage, covered with metal foil and completely bug-proof. Nothing, absolutely nothing can get in or out of this room. You can only enter the work area with a special access code and password." Don Rosso offered him a seat.

"My dear Karl, I am not sure if Marian has already told you about our traditions. It is simply a formality, but we still need to adhere to it. It is common in our circles that a prospective son-in-law asks the father for the hand of his daughter. I expect you to make up for that today. As a future spouse of my only daughter you will play an important role in our family. I would be very pleased if you would take this part in the same sincere and earnest way as my ancestors and I did." Don Rosso looked closely at Karl literally absorbing his emotions. The tension was written on both men's faces.

Then Karl smiled at him and the noticeable tension faded a bit. Don Rosso made himself a bit more comfortable in his large leather chair. There was no doubt that he was the boss, as he had been all his life. His natural behavior alone communicated this automatically to others.

Karl had crossed his legs and rocked one leg back and forth nervously. He was still very tense and was waiting for what Don Rosso had to tell him.

"My dear Karl, as you already know, we are quite a wealthy family. We have a variety of interests in renowned companies all around the world. Up till now I have managed everything together with a few confidants." Here Don Rosso paused briefly in order to analyze Karl's reactions again in detail.

Then he continued, "I am now getting on in years and it's all starting to get a bit much for me. Therefore I need a very trustworthy person who will assist me in my duties. However, regardless of how you decide, I must be sure you will treat this totally confidential. You may never tell anyone a single word about this, not even your wife. Karl, this is absolutely essential! It's a matter of survival! Can I rely on you?" Now, both men looked at each other with serious looks on their faces.

Karl thought that Don Serjo Rosso might be exaggerating a bit when he said that this was a matter of survival. There was no way he could even guess what bond of secrecy he was being committed to.

Only a few weeks later would he be able to understand that Don Rosso had spoken true words. Regardless of who it was who violated the codex of confidentiality, regardless of why this betrayal took place and what weight it carried, it always ended with the death sentence for the traitor that was carried out within a short period of time.

A huge map of the world hung directly behind Don Rosso's chair. It was packed with needles that had heads of different colors. Focus was on Europe and the United States. The boss saw Karl's confused look when he saw the map and told him that the needles symbolized part of the company investments of the family and the colors emphasized the focal points.

Karl heard Don Rosso's powerful voice. "So can I be absolutely and irrevocably sure about your loyalty to the family and that, no matter what happens in your future life, you will not pass anything on to others?" Don Rosso looked sternly at Karl with a questioning look on his face.

"I thank you, dear father-in-law, I assure you of my absolute confidentiality for all time."

Karl knew that with this sentence he had found exactly the right words that Don Rosso had wanted to hear him say.

The new member of the family was stunned by the assets

"Alright then. With that, you have become a member of our family and that's the way it will remain until the end of your life. It is also tradition that you show your respects at family gatherings by kissing my hand. I know, this is actually somewhat out of date, but in Sicily it is still part of the culture. So I need your commitment that you will do this just like the others do." he continued.

"My dear Karl, you are looking at the map of the world, these are our company investments which you are to control and manage in future for the benefit of our family. The whole thing needs to be completely reviewed and restructured. Everything has developed very successfully over the decades, but," Don Rosso cleared his throat, "because of my age, it's all slowly becoming too much for me. You have to take on this role and safeguard everything for our families."

Thoughts flashed wildly through Karl's mind. There must be a huge fortune behind it all, an incredible fortune! It was only the world's finest company names that were noted on the small flags that were attached to the colored needles. He had already believed in the tremendous financial strength of the family, but this was a truly unimaginable capital. Unbelievable that this could be hidden to a large extent from the public.

With his powerful voice Don Rosso explained, "We don't want to draw any unnecessary attention from the public to us. We have a lot of asset managers who are working for us. Everything is so deeply interlaced that not even the managers and lawyers know all of us as owners. And that is the way it should stay in the future. What you have to do is operate in the shadows. That is why we need confidentiality and the bug-proof room that, apart from you and me, only a few are allowed to enter. Your future wife will never get to see this room."

Now Karl understood the whole situation. It was also clear to him that that it had been easy for Don Rosso to convince the director of his bank to give him time off.

The assurance for confidentiality and the bug-proof room also made sense now. Karl had figured it out and he understood what this was all about. He felt a bit dizzy because the huge dimension of the family empire was not something that he had expected.

Don Rosso continued, "We could do politics with these company investments. Yes, we could conquer entire states. We could occupy whole countries with embargoes and delivery blockades thereby influencing local politics decisively. It will be your task to align the new network and monitor our administrators. Is that something you could imagine doing, Karl? Can you handle it?"

Karl replied, "I think so, but this is all happening so fast, I would like to ask for a short break. So I can think the whole thing through again. Just to be sure. Let's walk through the park a bit to try and relax."

Karl knew he was prolonging Don Rosso's tension thereby torturing him a bit. However, he needed a few minutes to calm his pounding head and gather his thoughts.

Pensively, they were strolling through the park when suddenly the butler came rushing towards Don Rosso. He whispered something in his ear that didn't seem to suit Don Rosso.

"Karl, I must interrupt our conversation briefly. Important business, you know. I will be back in an hour. The car, quick!"

One mistake could lead to a deadly war

Don Rosso rushed off. This was not inconvenient to Karl - he had a lot to think about.

Francesco welcomed Don Rosso with the usual kiss on the hand as a signal of respect. The two men stood at the edge of the cliffs watching the ocean waves. The men met maybe once a year. Francesco was the only one in the entire network who, apart from the first rank, had personal contact with the boss. He only received special orders from him to eliminate undesired people.

Francesco was a sniper and a true specialist in his field. He never made any mistakes and never left even the slightest traces behind. Moreover, he had no contact with other members of the Mafia.

"The messengers have already sent new to me in advance. How could this happen?", asked the boss, looking angrily at Francesco.

Messengers were the people in the organization that transported coded messages. Each of these messages was re-encrypted. One messenger brought the news, while another brought the encryption method to the destination address. In order to sharpen security, there were intermediate messengers. Neither the destination address nor the sender should be recognizable to the individual recipients at any time.
Just when everything was going so well with his daughter and Karl and Don Rosso was feeling close to his goal, he received a bad message.

"In all the years, this has never happened before. Are you getting too old for the job?" Don Rosso asked with furrowed brow.

Francesco replied sheepishly, "All of a sudden after the shot, the beam of a very low-flying airplane hit me. A landing light and the Chinese looked straight up at me." Francesco paused, before continuing with new strength. "But I am not sure, no, I don't think they recognized me because my face was covered anyway." However, Francesco looked somewhat uncertain while giving the explanation.

The boss passed his hands over his face. His features were marked with concern. "If they had caught on to even the slightest thing or become suspicious, war will rage. You know that." "It will all go well. Maybe I should clear off for a year and go to my lonely island", Francesco answered looking at his boss with a questioningly.

"You can't, Francesco! Damn it! I will have an urgent task for you soon, and maybe even a second one." Don Rosso was thinking now about a traitor in the network who had been identified and thrown out. He had sent the traitor under a pretext to Africa, to one of the jungles, as he called it.
Without him knowing that he had been discovered. The traitor was being observed continuously and had no opportunity to contact others unnoticed. But it wasn't the right time to get rid of the devious blabbermouth yet.

"Francesco, you know the Chinese will move heaven and hell to find out who has killed one of their clan bosses. They know no morals! They shoot first and don't care how many fall by the wayside. Even I, despite my contacts, could not protect you. I would have to worry about myself and my family." Desperately Don Rosso shook his head and looked at Francesco.

"It's all right. It was my mistake and if necessary, I will take the blame and pay for it." Don Rosso saw how worried Francesco was. "First, you should go to Germany for a while, to Dusseldorf. That's the last place they will look for you, just in case." Don Rosso shook Francesco's hand and set out on his return journey.

When he got back to the villa very much later than expected Karl looked at him questioningly but Don Rosso only said, "Karl, we need to continue our conversation tomorrow. I am too tired and want to rest a bit." He went into his rooms and was not seen again until the next day.

Unusually late, Marian's father came to the park the next day noticing how happy and in high spirits she was playing bocce with Karl. The loud laughter of the couple made his heart rejoice and his black thoughts disappeared just a little bit.

Nevertheless, he said a bit gruffly, "Good morning everyone! Karl, let's continue with our conversation!" The two of them returned to the house and back into the bug-proof conference room in silence.

"Your decision, Karl?" "I want to accept the job and make the most of it as far as I possibly can for the family!" Karl took Don Rosso's right hand and showed his respect with a Sicilian kiss on the hand.

Shortly after, Karl plucked up courage to ask, a little awkwardly and formally, Don Rosso for his daughter's hand in marriage,. With a short and crisp "yes" the father allowed him to take his daughter as his wife.

"Very well, very well, my dear son-in-law, thank you. But never forget to maintain your silence. We want to leave it at that today and tomorrow we will go straight to work. I now also have to prepare the wedding. But Marian can do that! Let's now relax for the rest of the day and celebrate a bit!"
Visibly relieved Don Rosso left the room and Karl followed him.

"My dear daughter, let your father be the first to congratulate you! Karl has just asked me for your hand in marriage and I of course agreed. I am so happy. We will give a lavish party! Isn't that wonderful news?" With joy, Marian jumped into Karl's arms and kissed him deeply. All three announced the good news to the staff and this didn't just spread throughout the house but also throughout the city in no time.

"Unfortunately, my daughter, you will have to handle the wedding preparations yourself,. Karl and I have a lot of business to do tomorrow." While saying this, Don Rosso furrowed his brow in a friendly way making the speech appear somewhat humorous.

Undaunted Marian replied, "Ok, you men. You will regret leaving me alone to do the preparations, but I wouldn't want to keep you business men back. I'll manage somehow."

During the next few days she worked tirelessly putting the guest list together and organizing the event with a few event managers. The estimated number of guests to be invited came to approximately 2000.

The church wedding was to take place only one day after the civil ceremony.. A white carriage with flowers was, of course, not to be forgotten. Over half of the business world living in Palermo was busy preparing for the wedding celebrations.

Karl intervened in the economy and was praised by Don Rosso

During the day, Karl and Don Rosso disappeared into the conference rooms to catalog the main company investments and managers. The sub-investments, i.e. the shares, which the companies had themselves, were completely unknown. Therefore, it was impossible to establish an exact register.

After Don Rosso had informed the administrators about Karl's extensive authority, Karl sent out a circular letter asking them to provide a complete list of all companies and company subparticipations.

At the same time Karl, ordered a stop for further investments by the managers and sub-managers. Exceptions were, of course, the banks from which they received shares., The purchase of shares up to the smallest company was terminated worldwide and loans were not to be granted.

Maybe this was also what caused the "black days" on international stock markets. But nobody learned of what the actual cause was and who was behind it.

Karl knew that this was a serious intervention. However, with the registering of the current status, he first wanted to gain an overview in ord to develop strategies for the future. He was also aware that this termination would not be allowed to last long, because the intervention would lead to a massive long-term impact on the international economy.

Therefore, he was working under high pressure and gave the managers and sub-managers only a very small time window for the cataloging.

The boss was very impressed by Karl's ambitious work and his systematic approach. The mutual trust grew steadily.

Karl spent the evenings only with his beloved Marian, who was making major progress with the planning of the wedding. The lovers worked hard and with great enthusiasm and everything was going fast so nothing could really go wrong.

Nevertheless, they were both forced to admit that such a large undertaking like their wedding was not something that could be arranged in two weeks. So they decided without further ado to postpone the wedding for another two weeks. But that didn't harm the happiness of the future spouses.

The wedding was a lavish celebration

Marian had prepared the motto "Sicilian Wedding". As the wedding day approached, the nervousness of the wedding couple increased. High-ranking guests from business and politics arrived from all parts of the world. Marian and her wedding planners provided accommodation for them in appropriate hotels.

A large stage and several huge circus tents were set up in the park. In the open spaces, wooden flooring had been laid out to make a dance floor. Several dozen people alone were busy with the seating. The wedding celebrations were to last for three days.

In the meantime, Karl established a to-do list that he wanted to work his way through in the coming weeks. One of the most important items on the list was to check out the main administrators and the accounts more closely. He could do this best by visiting the administrators and performing an on-site inspection.

Finally the time had come. The civil ceremony was to take place on the next day with a small circle of the closest friends. The couple had decided that it would make more sense to choose the common surname Rosso. This would also simplify future business affairs.

After the official ceremony, the wedding festivities with the honorable guests began on the grounds of the Rosso park. The guests' classy limousines drove up and as soon as the guests had stepped out of their vehicles, these were driven by reception staff to a spacious, landscaped parking lot. A band played traditional songs from Sicily. Everything went true to the motto "Sicilian Wedding".

A receptionist was standing next to the newlyweds and announced the guests by name. There was no end to the welcoming and shaking of hands and the lines of people did not cease when Marian suddenly felt faint in the hot afternoon sun. Karl and a member of staff escorted the bride into the house. There she stayed for a time resting from the strain.

Don Rosso and Karl took over the greeting of the guests for her and asked them politely for their understanding. After a while, the bride came back to the park and continued chatting with the guests.

As the guests were eating, the band played dance music. The newlyweds danced their wedding waltz in full view of all the guests. Everyone was enthusiastic about the lovely couple, Karl in a black tuxedo and the bride in her lovely pink dress.

To Karl's surprise, Marian also had invited the board member of the bank where Karl had previously worked. The bank director gave him the latest news from the bank.

In the late evening, the newlyweds said goodbye to the guests. As soon as they reached their room, they fell dead tired on the bed. However, the departure of the newlyweds didn't spoil the party and the guests continued celebrating into the early hours of the morning.

"What a great party, my dear," Karl said, and could barely keep his eyes open. "Yes, let's go to sleep, tomorrow the festivities will continue and it will be a long day. Thank you, my sweet husband and sleep well." One last kiss and the bride's eyes closed.

Early the next morning the bride's father and her husband to be sat on the terrace and waited hours for the bride. Several of the staff members and a make-up artist were preparing Marian for her big day.

In Catholic Sicily, a church wedding is still the most important day of a wedding celebration. On this day, Marian wanted to say yes to Karl's marriage proposal wearing a white dress with a long train. As she walked along the terrace towards Don Rosso and Karl she looked like an enchanting princess. Karl could not believe how beautiful Marian looked in her white wedding dress. It left him speechless and the bride's father could barely hold back his happiness. The bride's late mother had been half-Asian, her facial features could be seen in Marian's face making her look even more delightful.
"You really are a perfect couple", said Don Rosso and disappeared into the house to hide his tears of happiness from the public. Karl thought briefly about how unfortunate it was that his mother had not lived to see this, she would have been so happy.

At 11.30 a.m., the wedding carriage decorated with white roses arrived. The ecstatic staff stood full of curiosity as the couple and Don Rosso boarded the carriage. The four white horses and the coachman in his black top hat presented a romantic picture.

After the doors of the carriage closed, the carriage and four occupants started off slowly with the sun, which was at its best, and the beautiful couple trying to outshine each other.

When the carriage arrived in front of the patriarchal cathedral in Palermo, the square was crowded with people. The cathedral, which was built in the 6th century by Pope Gregory I, formed the dignified setting for this festival with its Arabic influences and the late Gothic portico. The square was decorated with colorful banners and flowers. It all looked like a royal wedding.

Karl got out of the carriage first and walked through the entrance to the altar. As they had practiced with the wedding planners, the bride's father followed the beat of the organ music and led the bride down the aisle past the guests to the altar.
Once there, he handed his daughter over to the groom. When the archbishop entered the cathedral, the choir in the nave began singing. The guests were all very touched by the ceremony. Some were so touched, they couldn't hold back their tears.

As the last act of the church ceremony, the archbishop asked the bride and groom to exchange rings.

After the groom had kissed the bride at the end of the ceremony, the newlyweds walked down the aisle to the exit followed by the bride's father and the invited guests. There, according to tradition, rice was thrown to give the couple good luck for life. The carriage with the newly wed bride and groom drove accompanied by the cheers of the spectators and the motorcade of the wedding guests followed them.

A lavish party took place together with all the invited guests in the villa complex. In the evening, a glittering and colorful firework display ended the festivities.

As they were finally undressing, Karl showered the woman of his dreams with kisses and caresses. He had been waiting all day for this moment. It was not much different for Marian. It was a long wedding night for the bride and groom that only ended in the early hours of the morning.

The cleanup work was already in progress when the happy couple appeared again the next afternoon. Even the bride's father was still a bit sleepy and groggy when they took their first cup of coffee together. Don Rosso mumbled in a scratchy voice, "A great party and a great success. The guests were all thrilled. You really are a dream couple. The photographers will show us the photographs tomorrow so that we can choose the best."

"Well, an event like that is quite tiring," Marian laughed and winked at Karl. "My dear husband is still in quite a daze and his hair is disheveled."

Don Rosso worked through a stack of newspapers where the wedding festivities were being highly praised. The Rosso family had presented themselves like this publicly for the first time ever. Karl also flipped through the newspapers only looking at the pictures as he was didn't feel fit enough to ready any of the texts yet because he was suffering from a bit of a headache.

"Will you be going on a honeymoon?" Don Rosso asked the couple. "Marian and I have decided to postpone this for a while so that we can recover a bit. In addition, I would also like to continue with my work in a few day's time," Karl said.

"Yes, just rest a bit and when you, Karl, are ready, we will continue with our work." As he was saying this, he nodded at Don Rosso in a favorable light.

The couple took two days off. They lay in the sun by the pool or played tennis. However Karl was itching to get back to his new job again. He decided to continue cataloging the shares of the company the next day.

"Serjo, I would like to continue with my work tomorrow, is that okay? Marian has agreed," Karl asked in order to forestall Don Rosso's question.The father replied, "That's convenient, I have urgent business I need to discuss with you."

He had been waiting the whole time for a sign from Karl that he ready to continue working. He could hardly wait because he was planning to finally teach his new right hand everything about the business including the Mafia organization. Don Rosso didn't want to wait any longer and finally get it behind him.

He had spent days and nights finding the right words. It now had to be pushed forward.

Early the next morning Don Rosso was pacing nervously through the park. He could hardly wait until Karl and Marian finally appeared. He made a mental note not to show his uncertainty.

The newlyweds arrived at the breakfast table in. "You will have to do without the best thing in your life for the next few days!", Marian exclaimed with a wide grin on her face. "I will visit Louisa, so that you can continue with your business undisturbed and I can talk about women's stuff again at long last."

Louisa was Marian's best friend and confidante and they had known each other for many years. "But not for long! Newlyweds should not be separated for long," replied Karl, obviously not quite liking the idea. Half an hour later, Marian said goodbye to her husband and father. The men disappeared into the working area of the villa.

"The records of the company shares have arrived from the managers from all corners of the world in the meantime, but before we look at these papers, I have some very important things I have to discuss with you. Please pay attention and listen closely to what I have to tell you," Don Rosso said to Karl.

After a vow of silence, the Mafia boss revealed himself

"My dear Karl, you will surely have given thought to how we were able to build up such a large fortune." Don Rosso paused briefly. Karl had in fact already wondered how it had been possible for the Rossos to accumulate such huge company assets. One time he had even noticed that in some of the banks and companies of the company network, cash flows of an unknown origin were flowing into the network. Karl had decided to ask Don Rosso what was causing this. He was sure that there was a simple explanation to this. It would never have occurred to him that this had something to do with illegitimate affairs.

"Karl, I have to warn you once again that not the slightest word is passed on to a third party. This is essential in order to survive. You are now a full member of our family." Both of them looked at each other stonily. Karl was a bit shocked about his father-in-law's important words, something that Don Rosso had noticed immediately. "My dear son-in-law, up until now you have only been informed about the legitimate company investments, but the way I judge you, you will probably have already asked yourself how we were able to accumulate this capital."

Don Rosso repeated this on purpose and then paused again briefly continuing then straight away, "I would now like to tell you everything! Karl, your father-in-law is the highest family member of the international Mafia." Don Rosso waited anxiously for Karl's reaction. "That's a good joke, Serjo! Really, a very good joke, even for this early in the morning." Karl laughed. However, he was not sure whether it really was just a bad joke or the frightening truth.

Don Rosso continued in a very serious voice, "Remember this for all time: there will be no jokes as long as we are sitting and talking in this room.. These matters are too serious. No! This is not a joke! This is the truth and you will be my successor and responsible for the family! I have big plans for the future."

Karl caught his breath. his fears about safety were just going through his head again. Cold sweat now appeared on his forehead. What kind of situation had he got himself here? Little Karl, organization manager of a bank with a condominium that was not yet paid for, sitting in front of the boss of the international Mafia? His heart raced and he was unable to say a single word at that moment.

"My big plan is to realign the Mafia organization and for this I need your help!" Karl wondered what in God's name he could contribute to this. What would Marian say about what her father had planned with her husband?
Finally, Karl was able to compose himself a bit and ask the burning question, "Then the cash inflow that I noticed and was unable to explain in some of the companies comes from Mafia money?" "Exactly, that's right. I thought you had noticed inconsistencies while you doing your work," Don Rosso replied.

"This is strong stuff! I have to digest this, let's go to

the park and have a drink." Karl looked at his father-in-law pleadingly while he was saying it. "But not a single word goes outside this secured room. Karl, never forget that! Okay, let's go to the park for half an hour and have a drink." Serjo went ahead and Karl followed him.

"Two whiskeys with ice or rather bring a whole bottle to the pool," Don Rosso called out to the butler. Karl downed the first glass without putting it down. That was exactly what he needed to revive a bit. Had he really heard what he had just heard or was this just a bad dream? Could Serjo really be a notorious Mafia boss? Don Serjo Rosso with his so serious reputation? From whom you would never have suspect a gangster boss behind it?

His father-in-law, who appears the very gentleman, with his excellent education and first-class upbringing? Could that really be correct? The father of his bride was an international crime boss? Somebody who probably had more lives on his conscience than anyone else on the planet?

Karl quickly poured himself another whiskey and drank it in a hurry. Don Rosso watched him with compassion, trying to understand Karl's feelings. Karl's mobile phone rang and he answered the call a bit confused, "Grosser. No sorry, my name is Rosso, good day! Hello Marian, yes I'm fine, we are simply very engrossed in our work and I am still a little confused, if you understand what I mean, my love. And you, what are you doing?"

"I didn't want to disturb your important work, I am with Louisa and we are having a lovely chat. But honestly, I miss you so much. I will introduce you to Louisa sometime soon, she's such a dear. Call me when you have time, see you later and a very big kiss, just for you, see you soon." She had already hung up.

Now a thousand questions raced through Karl's head at the same time. How were these transactions done? How were they organized? Why did no one actually notice anything about the business that was taking place here so quietly? Questions, questions, question, but no answers for the moment. Less than half an hour had passed when Don Rosso said, "Come on, let's go back to work!"

Although his life was dear to him, Karl had reached the point of no return

Now Karl saw his father-in-law in a new light. This friendly, elderly gentleman with his elegant outward appearance. Always impeccably, but inconspicuously dressed. Was it all just a trick to hide behind his true and brutal self? How could a man be so divided? On the one hand act like the loving father on the outside, someone who was always friendly to everyone while in reality he was a brutal gangster boss? A gentleman who probably kept a gun in his jacket pocket and was ready to use it at any time to kill people.

The old movies about the Mafia that he had seen in the movie theaters now buzzed around in Karl's head. Brutal shootings that always cost countless lives. But here everything was different. Here, the organization of the worldwide Mafia was operating quietly and totally unnoticed by the outside world hidden behind serious facades. Don Rosso was pulling all the strings. Who were the other bosses who he had not seen yet? Could he or did he even want to work together with these gangster bosses?

It was clear to him that there was now no way to back out of this again. His life would probably not be worth a cent anymore. He was sure that even though Karl was married to his daughter, Don Rosso wouldn't hesitate to get rid of a disloyal confidant.

What could he do? Although he was not comfortable with the situation, there was no escape. He had to go along with it whether he wanted or not. In that regard, despite all the unease, he was happy that he would not need to make his own decision anymore. But how would the situation progress? And what did his father-in-law mean with the realignment of the organization?

As they entered the secured room again, Don Rosso explained in his distinctive voice, "You are the first and only person who learns about my reorganization plans beforehand! The families have to be led into a secure future, that is why this reorganization is urgently required. You are sure to have had a different opinion of our organization until now. We have not been the trigger-happy Mafia that most people know from old movies for a long time now. Our grandfathers certainly started out like that at one time. But these days we are doing everything in a much more subtle way." Don Rosso took a deep breath in order to continue his monologue. "First, you have to learn how our organization is structured and networked."

Don Rosso told him about the three ranks and his ancestors, how his fathers and ancestors had built up the Mafia family and started out first with a small group in Palermo in order to then capture Europe and the United States. He described in detail the network set up by the ancestors with the structure of the inner ranks up to the so-called messengers who brought encrypted messages to various destinations without knowing both the starting point and the address of the destination at the same time.

Finally, he informed his son-in-law about the cash flows that were fed into the network via money laundering operations. In insignificant companies, sales were faked and invoiced or various accounts supplied with cash assets from corrupt banks. The earnings were then passed through several companies and used to purchase company shares. This happened in such a way that no one could understand the process or identify the strategy behind it.

Just as the day was drawing to a close and Karl's brain started to feel as if it would burst with the amount of information that filled it, the big boss said, "I think we have worked enough for today. Tomorrow is another day. You have to process first what you have learned today."

That was for sure. Karl first had to take it all in. He still had a lot of questions. He would have liked to have heard even more about the Mafia's plans for the future, but he also welcomed a break.

Karl spent the evening by the pool pondering and he let the day's events run through his mind again. Then he decided to sleep for a while and he retreated to the bedroom.

All of a sudden, machine guns rattled around him. Bullets flew through the air. Loud screams. A bomb exploded with a huge bang. The air smelt of burned gunpowder. People fell to the ground screaming and writhing in pain. Some were still trying to escape from the death squad. Karl plucked up his courage and grabbed one of the guns lying near him. He killed dozens of opponents fearlessly using the automatic rifle. The tires of the getaway car screeched. He was the admired hero and savior of the community.

Then he heard Don Rosso, who was patting him on the shoulder say to him, "Well done, my fearless Karl. Yes, you are my real son-in-law."

Karl woke up bathed in sweat. It took a while until he realized that this had all just been a dream. His heart was pounding hard as if to say that he had reached the limits of his ability to handle stress. He looked at his watch nervously. It was still early in the morning and everyone in the villa was still asleep.

However, after this horrible dream he was unable to sleep another wink. He lay awake in bed, lost in his thoughts. After a while, he went into the bathroom to recover from the shock and take a refreshing shower.

After he had dressed, he crept through the house quietly. The deadly silence in the villa seemed sinister now. He only felt a bit more at ease after the domestic workers took up their work again. He went to the pool and swam a few laps. That was the very thing to relax after such a night.

Don Rosso was also up and about particularly early that day, "Hi Karl, are you fit? Did you have a good night's sleep?"

Karl retorted, "It was a short night for me, Serjo. There were so many things going through my mind."

Don Rosso looked at him and saw that Karl looked a bit sleepy, "I thought it was all a bit much yesterday. Shall we start working again in two hour's time?"

"That's okay, I would just like to talk to Marian beforehand," Karl replied. After an extensive phone conversation with Marian, Karl and the Don starting working. Again, they took their places at the long conference table that was made out of old oak wood.

Without hesitating Don Rosso continued where he had stopped the day before, "So, we now have corporate interests in the best and biggest companies of the world. Profit distributions already make up a large amount of our revenue. We could in theory all live well from this. With that I mean all the family member, those from the first rank and their relatives."

"I can imagine," Karl interjected. "but surely you also have other major sources of revenue? What kind of a plan have you worked out for the future of the Mafia? And how can I contribute to it?"

"I'm afraid I can't tell you the details at this point in time. But you play an important role in my planning. This will take many years to complete. What can you contribute? That question is absolutely justified! The project is huge. And this is exactly why I need your help. I have planned a period of about five to seven years for its implementation. Everything should be completed by 2020. That is enough time to see this through carefully."

"This has been planned very farsightedly. What will my job be here?" Karl looked blankly at Don Rosso.

"You can help me with many things, Karl. On the one hand, with the organization of the company shares and controlling the managers. On the other hand also with a specific task. We must work together to convince the members of the first rank who have not yet been informed that it is now time to reach new horizons. That will certainly be a difficult task. The plan can only succeed if we can convince them all and the members stand behind it united. If only one single member of the first rank does not participate, we can forget the whole plan."

This was clear to Karl even without knowing the details.

"We will hold a general meeting for all members of the first rank in the coming weeks. This alone will already be a major organizational task. Up until now, because there are so many precautions that have to be taken, we only got together for a general meeting every five years. You never know what a chief of police has maybe noticed about one or the other member."

Don Rosso looked very thoughtful while explaining. He continued his monologue, "I know I am asking a lot of you now, but this is really necessary. We must after all in future take care of the members of the first rank and their families so that they also can live a good life. This is the long-term responsibility that we have to carry. Can you accept this inheritance?"

Karl looked at him still somewhat uncertain and replied, "I never expected to ever be given such a huge responsibility in my whole life, but I realize that I have to accept the inheritance. I will exert all my energy to accomplish this task as well as possible. I promise you, father-in-law! "

Even though there were still a lot of detailed questions that arose for Karl, this took a weight off Don Rosso's mind and he was excited about his son-in-law's vow. Deep from his soul he said, "That's just great, we must celebrate this. Karl, give Marian a call and tell her she should come back quickly, after all, she has left us alone long enough and Louisa is a pure substitute for such two strong guys like us."

The boss was obviously in a partying mood. He had carried this burden around with him for long enough. Now he was all the more relieved.

"A good idea, Serjo, I will call her. I have to admit, I am already missing her very much."

Karl went to the door together with Don Rosso, and when they reached the park, he pulled out his cell phone from his pocket and dialed his wife's phone number.

"Hello darling, how are you? I hear engine noise, where are you now?" Karl was a little surprised when he heard road noise in the background from Marian's side.

"I wanted to surprise you! Well, unfortunately I failed, I will be with you in ten minutes. I couldn't wait, I have missed you so much."

Marian had not really been able to concentrate on her discussions with Louisa. She kept thinking about her beloved all time, wondering how he was getting on with her father. Marian knew her father well and knew that he could also be very rude if something didn't fit in with his plans, but fortunately that only happened very rarely.

Karl told Don Rosso straight away that his wife was already on her way back to the villa.

"That's good, then we can have lunch together in the restaurant 'Don Camillo' at the small fishing harbor. The owner, Pedro, is an old friend of the family. There you get the best fresh fish in all of Palermo."

Don Rosso was beaming and you could tell by his expression that the world was now perfect for him.

The best fish platter couldn't hold back the assassins

No sooner had Marian arrived, did her father insist driving straight to the harbor. As the security men had to be present all the time, they took two cars. "Greetings, Pedro, long time no see! How's your family doing?", Don Rosso greeted his old friend and owner of the restaurant. Bowing over, Pedro took Don Rosso's right hand kissed it with respect.

"Everything is going really well. My daughter has had her second baby, the whole family is proud of her. But I have already heard that Marian got married. This news has spread throughout the city fast," the delighted Pedro said.

"This is my son-in-law," Don Rosso introduced Karl to him. "a splendid fellow, I could not imagine a better one."

Pedro welcomed the young couple warmly, "Marian and Karl, welcome to my humble inn. How nice that I get to know your husband at last, dear Marian. To celebrate the day, I will serve the best fish that you have ever eaten in your whole life."

Pedro clapped his hands and called out to his staff, "Wine for my friends, but only the best."

It was a pretty little restaurant with blue awnings. The tables were set very nicely and on each table there was a vase filled with a small bunch of flowers.

From the terrace you could watch the hustle and bustle of the fishermen with their nets. The midday sun was still very hot, only the fans on the walls generated a bit of cool air. "What a lovely place," Karl said.

They drank a deep red wine and were just trying a few delicious appetizers when a small black car drove up with screeching tires. Two young guys with black balaclavas jumped out of the still moving vehicle. The Rossos' bodyguards had positioned themselves in front of the table and drawn their two pistols at a flash. They were not participating in the activities underneath the terrace, but were making sure that the Don and his family were safe.

The men held guns in their hands and ran over to one of the younger fishermen. One held the fisherman tight while the other one shot him in the back of the head. The fisherman fell to the ground covered in blood. Everything happened so quickly that no one was able to intervene. The killer ran back to the car and raced off.

Karl looked horrified and questioningly at his father-in-law who suppressed his question with a dismissive gesture.

A few minutes later, a siren and the flashing lights of approaching police cars could be perceived. By the time they arrived, the square was already deserted. Through fear of being questioned by the Commissarios, everyone had disappeared very quickly. Two police officers arrived on the terrace of the restaurant and greeted Don Rosso and the young couple casually. "Can you tell us anything about the murder," asked one of the officer, looking first at Don Rosso then at Karl and finally at the terrified Marian.

Serjo's voice now sounded as cold as ice to Karl. "We hardly saw anything. We only noticed something after the first shot went off and by then the escape vehicle was already rushing away. Everything went so quickly that we couldn't even see the number plate. The guys wore black masks. Unfortunately, I or rather we are not able to say anything. This is a very sad state of affairs." Don Rosso showed no emotions whatsoever.

The Commissario replied, "Very annoying, but it's like this every time. By the time we arrive, everyone has disappeared and no one has seen anything. All that is left for us is to remove the bodies. But no offense, Don Rosso, and have a nice day, I have your address should we have any questions."

"I hope you have not lost your appetite. This is unfortunately the dark side of Palermo. This happens all the time here on Sicily. This is something you have to accept, unfortunately. But, don't let it spoil your party mood. We will have a wonderful meal here." Don Rosso acted as if nothing had ever happened.

Karl was a bit surprised at his father-in-law's callousness but he quickly turned to his beloved wife who was very clearly terrified and sat like a statue on her chair. He took her hand and kissed it gently hoping to be able to calm Marian down a bit.

A short time later, Pedro served a huge seafood platter that contained all sorts of different seafood. Don Rosso eat heartily and his daughter recovered quickly from the shock. Karl thought about how everyone had behaved after the incident. What was particularly noticeable was the behavior of those who had not been directly involved and who behaved as if nothing had happened. Obviously, no one wanted to take notice that a murder had just happened in front of their eyes.

While they had been eating the fresh fish with salad and vegetables, the police had completed their formalities underneath the terrace and a hearse had removed the dead body.

After the officers left, the forecourt of the harbor filled straight away again with a lively crowd. Karl was puzzled at the strange way the people dealt with a murder. The way everybody was carrying on with their evening as usual, it was as if this would a matter of course.

A while later, as the three of them were spending their evening together on the terrace of the villa to bring the day to an end, Don Rosso said to Karl, "Tomorrow your beloved Marian has to spend the day on her own. Duty calls." Marian showed understanding, "Of course I understand, that's not a problem for me."

The next morning, the boss and his son-in-law went straight back to the office area of the villa. Karl was still a bit confused by the events of the previous day and asked Don Rosso, "What did the shootings yesterday at the harbor mean?"

His father-in-law replied evasively, "Well, I really can't say precisely. I suspect the deceased has broken his vow of silence or stolen from the Mafia. But that is not our business. The 2nd or 3rd ranks have to deal with that, without my involvement. I could find out what was behind it but we don't want to waste our time doing that.! How far did you get with the stocktaking of our company investments?"

Karl introduced a new surveillance software

Karl reported, "I have received all the information from the trustees and this has I have entered today into a computer program. And I have resumed business activities. All granting of credits or new investments through our companies will now be reported to me immediately through our trustees. The nature and scope of all company investments of one million and above will be reported to me. Anything above $ 10,000,000 will first require my approval. Thus we will be able to determine the nature and scope of our company investments at any time of day or night. In addition, we will be able to develop strategies regarding which companies or products we should invest in internationally to get better market strength. I think that will be our next step."

Then he continued, "But I have another concern or rather an idea. I am thinking about installing a computerized controlling system in all companies. That would help to have direct access to the companies."

Don Rosso looked at Karl questioningly, "Explain that to me in more detail please, how does that work in practice?"

Karl described this euphorically, "That is relatively easy. All companies are asked by the trustees to implement a so-called management software tool. That means the companies install a program in addition to their financial software. With this, we have direct access to the companies."

Don Rosso thought about this for a moment and was convinced, "That's a great idea. I knew you were the right person for this. It's all even better than I ever imagined it could be. What is also important is that there is no traceable link back to us. You are excluded from this and can officially manage things as you please. But your name should not leak to the outside more than is absolutely necessary. You should rather remain invisible and work together with the trust companies." He looked at Karl in order to make sure that he understood what he was saying. Then he continued, "And it really works so easily? Tell me more! Will the companies not realize that we are observing their activities?"

"Don't worry, Serjo! That will be prevented! The system will of course include strictly confidential confirmation requests in order to be able to even enter it."

Karl walked over to the flipchart and wrote down a few examples on the large-sized paper, "You see, this is the remote company with the financial software. A so-called standardized software tool will now be added to this software. With the help of the management tool, the information is shared internally on the company's computer. The exchange takes place without human intervention, fully automatic."

"Stop, Karl, wait, my head is already hurting! These young people with their EDP systems. An old man like me can't follow this so quickly," Don Rosso warned.

"I don't think you have to worry about this in detail," Karl calmed him. "In any case, three dongles are supplied with the management tool. These are for the questions of authenticity for identification and authorization. Whoever has this has access to the software and data. One dongle for the company head himself, two for the trustee who will provide us one under his name." Karl drew another diagram for better understanding.

Proudly the boss realized, "I see! We get one of those gadgets and it helps us to access the company."

"Exactly, we can log in using the dongle that we get from the trustee and access the company directly. And if the company is fit enough technology-wise, the only thing it can detect is that someone has logged into the software. However, since the company only knows about the two dongles that the trustee has, there is no way of determining that we have accessed the system. Have I been able to explain that to you in an understandable way? I can explain it to you in more detail later," Karl offered.

"I have understood everything so far. But is this really 100% safe? Does our identity really remain undetected and how big is the effort? That all sounds very complicated and time-consuming." Don Rosso looked at Karl doubtfully.

"It probably sounds complicated, but it's not. It doesn't cost much more effort than the installation of another software program on the computer. Only those who have the dongle can access the system and it looks like any other normal flash drive that you insert into a computer. It is 100% safe!" Karl radiated a unique confidence.

"That's good Karl. No, it's *great*. And it also saves us a whole lot of travel expenses. Karl, you are great and priceless. Your bank probably had no idea how clever you really are." Don Rosso was already thinking even a bit further and was certain that he could use this to monitor monies received. This way, he had an instrument to check the money-laundering operation at the same time.

It had often been his problem that he was only able to check the inflow of money at a very late point in time, if at all. After handing over the money, people definitely had the opportunity of putting something in their own pockets and announcing a smaller amount of money as the takings. That had been a thorn in the boss' side for a long time already. However, he didn't want to discuss that with his son-in-law at this point.

Karl felt very flattered by his father-in-law's praise. You could see how proud it made him.

"Father-in-law, if you don't mind, I will begin with the process tomorrow and advise our administrators in writing." Even though he was sure that Don Rosso would agree, he still wanted his consent again.

"Yes, do that. I don't think we begin fast enough. How long will it take until everything is ready?" Don Rosso asked.

Karl replied, " I'm not exactly sure, I reckon with three to four, maximum six months until everything has been implemented."

"That's enough for today, it's already past 6 o'clock, we've done a lot today. Let's eat something and enjoy the evening . We have been so busy today that we haven't even had lunch. Tomorrow we will deal with the big family gathering. That will be a lot of work. Let's go!" Don Rosso started to move.

"Lo and behold! My men are back at last. Did you have a nice and busy day?" asked Marian amused herself as the two of them finally appeared on the terrace.

"We did a great job, your Karl is the greatest of all! Tomorrow we will continue straight away," Don Rosso praised his son-in-law.
Karl turned to Marian and said a bit meekly, "Hello my darling, please forgive me, we have been so busy that we forgot the time. But now I am really hungry."

The three had a happy dinner and drank a fruity red wine in the twilight.

At 10 o'clock the next day Don Rosso and Karl were already back in the conference room engrossed in their conversation.

"Father-in-law, I have thought of something else! We could shift the costs for the new software to our company network. If the companies in which we hold a major stake hire a software company that I have already chosen, the costs will simply be shifted. The profits will remain with us in full." Karl's eyes gleamed expectantly and he secretly hoped to gain further praise from his father-in-law.

"Yes, my dear son-in-law, what else can I say? I agree with that. Excellent idea! Then it costs us nothing. You really do have everything under control," Don Rosso agreed.

"I have known the software house for many years already and so far they have always been totally reliable. They are certainly not a particularly large company, but they are capable of doing the job and they do it to our full satisfaction. If you don't mind, I will immediately issue a written order to the trustee companies so that they can forward this on to the companies."

Don Rosso had no objection, "Good idea, then they should start with the order right away. But Karl, please keep out of it otherwise and only place the order. Our trust companies or the companies themselves will take care of everything else. Even though you are only responsible for legitimate business, we do not want you to appear so much in public. You will soon learn why that is so important to me."

Meanwhile, Don Rosso had been busy rummaging around in documents and he spread out a large world map on the long conference table and bent over it.

The meeting of the international bosses had to be planned

"Karl, now we will deal with the family reunion. First, we must decide where we are going to hold the meeting! I am thinking of Germany, somewhere in the area of Dusseldorf. There are plenty of cities and airports there. We should plan five days for the actual meeting. That should be enough."

As he was talking, he looked at the map a bit aimlessly. "It's very convenient that the family members all went to the residential school in Switzerland. We all learned German there which is an advantage. All the members of the first rank speak Italian, German and English."

"A whole week for one meeting?" Karl asked.

Don Rosso replied, "Yes, we're all not the youngest any more! That's why we'll book the hotels for two weeks as a precaution. Everybody gets a suite, they can also bring their wives and children with them. The whole thing will be arranged with a maximum of safety, my dear. Therefore, we will chose a different venue for every day and these will only be known to the two of us beforehand. We will accommodate the ten family members of the first rank in different cities and hotels. On the meeting days, they will be picked up by chauffeurs. It's extremely risky bringing all the bosses together at once. If only one is careless, the cover of the entire organization could be blown away through the surveillance actions of the police and judiciary system. This must be ruled out."

Don Rosso paused and filled two glasses with water. He drank hastily and was tense. While he was doing that, he kept turning the heavy letter opener that was always lying on the conference table.

"We need large conference rooms in hotels with multiple access routes. That means with an elevator that leads directly to the underground parking garage. You have to ask about that. Regardless of costs. We need seven conference rooms. Our mobile and bug-proof conference cage must be installed on the premises in the mornings. I will give you the names of the people who will arrange that for us. And now, let's get to work, I need to work out the travel routes for the members and you will look for the hotels."

Don Rosso went to his big old oak desk and pottered about busily with the world map. First he entered the locations of the first rank members onto the map, followed by connecting lines to Germany.

Karl searched about on the internet for suitable hotels with conference rooms and made a list of names and addresses. A further list included the hotels in the different cities that were available as accommodation for the family members.

Without Don Rosso asking him to do this, Karl planned trips for the wives during the meeting times. Karl's father-in-law approved of this far-sightedness a lot.

Suddenly Don Rosso exclaimed, "Oh, I almost forgot! The whole thing is disguised as a shareholder meeting of the company La Finette AG. This is a company in Paris! All family members hold shares of this company. I actually wanted to surprise you later with this, but we will make it short. You are now the new second board member of this company. Your office has already been set up directly on the beautiful Champs-Élysées. I was thinking you really can't remain an employee of the bank forever. Anyway, your salary is 900,000 Euros . I hope that's enough!" The boss laughed. "And when you have time, fly there for a few days. Take a look at the balance sheets, and then the people there will have seen you too. Your wife will be happy to accompany you. She loves Paris more than any other place. Oh yes, your should prepare a friendly letter of resignation for your current employer."

Karl was delighted, "I am speechless! You really forget nothing. Many, many thanks, father-in-law. I must tell Marian about this later on."
"Yes, later, but let's get back to work now. I have set the first day for the meeting for in three month's time, on the 23rd of July. The gentlemen can then rest in the hotel from the journey for three days beforehand." This is what the boss had decided.

The overall planning and organization of the meeting took several days. As usual, the hotel and conference rooms were booked by the large lawyer's firm in downtown Palermo. The next step was to organize the travel routes for the members. The flights were arranged not as direct flights, but with stopovers. Not even the members were informed about the actual meeting location or the travel routes. They would only know the next destination and find the necessary tickets when they got to the hotel rooms at their stopovers.

"A little lavish," Don Rosso said to Karl. "but nevertheless necessary to be very sure that no one really knows where our meeting takes place. The members already know that and agree because it serves for the safety of all of us. Now, let us have a closer look at the personal data of the members so that you, Karl, also get to know the people. You have already seen them for the most part at your wedding, but their true identity was still hidden from you back then. It was not yet the right time to inform you."

Karl was very attentive and curious now. He was finally to get to know the players of the honorable family. "Everyone has a nickname. First, we have *Fast Giuseppe*, he organizes the transfer of funds. A very important and absolutely reliable man. He collects the cash receipts and is responsible for ensuring that the money flows into the legal loop. But more on that later.
Next, you see *Exact Davide*, he is responsible for the organization in the USA. A very sly fox. Then we have *Beautiful Filippo*, who is actually quite ugly, but he is always happy when someone refers to him as beautiful. He is responsible for the unpleasant to us, but necessary drug business.

Nicole is responsible for the Asian region. The situation there is getting increasingly difficult for us. *Diego* is fighting for us on the African market and *Antonio* monitors our business in Europe. *Luca* is responsible exclusively for our casinos, especially in Las Vegas. *Fine Michele* is only active in lobby work with politicians all over the world. He costs us a fortune, but thanks to him we have access to the major players in politics. *Eduardo* is the uncrowned king of Italy and last but not least, we have the *Charming Marco*, who specifically takes care of the protection money.

"You see, my dear Karl, we are very well positioned. Although, the structure has grown and is no longer typical, we have everything under control. Our people are the best in their field." As he finished the sentence, he leaned back leisurely in his desk chair and added, "The only direct contacts that I personally cultivate are the ones with the supremos of the Russian families and the Triad boss of the Chinese. This is essential for us."

It was absolutely quiet in the room now and you could hear a pin drop. After some time, Karl took a deep breath. He began, "It is unbelievable that this has functioned for decades without the public noticing anything about it." "That's correct. But we are also working meticulously so that no prying journalists or cops suss out what we are doing. However, if somebody should get too close, then ..." Here the boss of all bosses broke off his sentence prematurely.

"Karl, during the next few days, please work out the exact meeting points and hotels and then give everything to our lawyer in Palermo. I must devote myself to my own business for a few days and also rest a bit.

You can have a closer look at the personal dossiers of the family members and their photos during a quiet moment."

Karl confirmed, "Okay, you can rely on me. Can we pack up work for today? I promised your daughter that we would finish a little earlier today and that we would have a game of tennis." "But of course, no problem. Tomorrow is another day and we have to pay tribute to our women. So, buzz off, I'll join you a bit later." As Don Rosso spoke these words, he stood up from his desk chair and turned the golden letter opener around on the conference table with pleasure.

A bit later Marian could be heard, "Out! Out! You have to practice a bit, my dear husband. But don't worry, that will come." Marian laughed at Karl because she had beaten him at tennis again. But it was also very funny how Karl could get annoyed when he lost. He had, of course, no chance against her. After all, she had tennis lessons every day.

Karl took his water bottle and shook some water in her direction, obviously frustrated and in despair. "This was a clear foul. You are going to pay for that tonight!" Marian called out to him and ran to her father who was lying beside the pool. It was pleasurable hearing the playful bantering between the two. "Daddy, my dear daddy. Are you okay?" She asked him. "Yes, my child. I feel great. When I see how positive our work is progressing, I feel better every day. Did your loser already tell you that he is now a member of the executive board in Paris?"

102

Marian replied, "Of course, he proudly delivered this news to me straight away. He also told me that we will soon fly together to Paris for a few days so that he can see that everything is running properly in the company . But he still has no chance against me at tennis." Karl took his time walking over from the tennis court gradually. Obviously also in order to get over his anger a bit without the others noticing. "Let's have dinner, then I'll go to bed, tomorrow is another busy day." With this, Don Rosso set an end to the bantering at the pool.

Marian had not just been threatening when she told Karl that he would have make amends that night. She had learned a lot during the lifetime of her marriage. In addition to the long working days, the nights had now also become very short for him.
The next morning while having breakfast Karl asked, "Marian, we could fly to Paris at the end of the week and stay there until Tuesday or Wednesday. Is that okay? Then I can have a look at my new executive chair and examine the books." She leapt with joy, "My sweetheart, I will be with you for the first time in the city of love, that will be fantastic! Romantic dinners together in cozy French restaurants. Yes ... "

Before she could finish the sentence, Don Rosso stood up and said, "Karl, come, let her continue dreaming. That will keep her busy today and we can get back to work again."

The two immediately disappeared and left Marian alone with her dreams.

They had to get rid of a turncoat with one move

Several messages lay on the desk and Don Rosso opened them skillfully with a letter opener. He took his time to decode the information and read it through. All of a sudden he yelled and leapt up from his chair, "Damn it! I don't believe it! That dirty scoundrel!" He was still holding the golden letter opener and raising his hand, he slammed it into the desk as hard as he could.

Karl was shocked. He had never seen Don Rosso so angry. The anger let the blood rush to his boss' head. It was hard to calm him down and he ran around like a tiger in a cage.

It was some time until Karl carefully asked for the cause of this sudden outburst, "Is something wrong? Is there trouble?"

"You can say that again! That bastard! Rogue! This will end his life! My patience has come to an end! I thought he would pull himself together again! But nothing of that! Now he went the whole hog! I must act quickly. Tomorrow I will fly to Dusseldorf! You will have to do without me for a few days." The boss got up and left the room.

Intimidated and thoughtful Karl was left alone in the office area. Two hours later Don Rosso returned in a noticeably bad mood. In the meantime, Karl had gone about his organization work. He didn't dare ask his father-in-law again what had got him so upset.

"I fly in an hour." Don Rosso now corrected his previous statement. "Every minute counts. I can't put it off. But please don't ask me anything now, Karl. I will tell you everything later. First of all I have to take care of the matter I'll see you tomorrow." He went and was not seen again that day.

Even Marian had noticed her father's bad temper and asked Karl what had happened when he joined her again in the park, "Bad news? Father left without saying a word."

"I don't know," Karl replied, putting her off with the wave of a hand.

During the evening of the same day Don Rosso landed at the private airport in Düsseldorf. He had arranged a meeting with Francesco.

Francesco was still worrying about the mishap that had happened to him as he tried to shoot the Chinese Mafia boss dead.

They both went for a walk in the forest. After a while, Don Rosso began, "Well, my dear man. Have you recovered? Everything seems to be going well. Even though the Chinese are still looking for you, from what I have heard, they have no suspicions against us."

Francesco replied, "Yes, everything seems to be fine. You can't even imagine how I have been brooding for the last few days. Something like that will never happen to me again. You can be certain, boss. Please forgive me!"

"Francesco, you have been a top man for decades, you are faithful and devoted. Mistakes can always happen. But that is not the reason why we meet today," Don Rosso replied. "That villain, Eduardo! The uncrowned king of Sicily. I had told you about him. As a precaution, I sent him to Africa, to the so-called jungle, on a pretext. There he was watched by my people day and night without noticing it. You know, so that he could do no harm." He wiped his hand over his sweaty forehead.

"The uncrowned king of Sicily? The one from the first rank?", Francesco asked surprised.

Gasping, the boss continued with short sentences, "Yes, that 's right, the idiot. I don't know what he is thinking. We spent our whole life together, he is doing well, our ancestors cared for us all. That arrogant idiot. Mamma mia !" Now a little bit of the Sicilian blood came through in Don Rosso. He could barely maintain his composure. This was not his style. But it was an exceptional situation here and that excused his behavior a bit. He added, "I can neither understand nor can I comprehend the real reason."

Understandably, Don Rosso could not hide his anger and he screamed out, "One of us! From our circle! Our own family member! That has never happened before! Tomorrow you will go straight to Johannesburg and settle the matter. But please, don't be soft! He should still get something out of it. I have already withdrawn our people who are watching him so you only have to deal with his two bodyguards. That should be not a problem for you, right?"

Without waiting for Francesco's answer he mused further, "If it had been someone from the 2nd or 3rd rank I could perhaps would have understood it. But from our own ranks." He paused for a moment and you could feel his despair even in the darkness.

"I understand," Francesco said. "It has to look like an accident, but it is supposed to be painful for him. Right?"

"Exactly! Yes, exactly! What can you offer me? It should be something special for him," Don Rosso wanted to know.

Francesco didn't hesitate, "Well, I am thinking of the special venom from Caracas. It will never be discovered that it was due to poisoning."

Don Rosso was satisfied, "That sounds good. And does it works without a big fuss?"

Francesco continued, "I have already used it. Do you remember that asshole from New York? The poison is undetectable, absolutely deadly and it drags out the victim's intestines for hours. The person is motionless but fully conscious. At the time, the doctors suspected an unknown viral infection."

Don Rosso interrupted Francesco before he could finish his detailed description, "Yes, that should be suitable for the bastard. Only one thing still worries me, his friends from the second rank. What do you think? I mean, the family should not know who is behind this. But they should not think that another group is responsible for this either, otherwise they could start a vendetta."

Francesco replied, "I have an idea. We let the whole thing look as if Eduardo has blotted the Chinese's copybook. We tell the Chinese that we have punished the turncoat and we keep our own ranks clean. Then both topics have been dealt with and the family as well as the second rank are left out of it." "Great idea!" The boss was delighted. "Surely we will be rewarded by the Chinese for this. That sounds very credible." After thinking about it for a while Don Rosso continued, "I will inform the top Asia boss about it as soon as the deed has been done. He will be a bit stubborn that he couldn't deal with Eduardo himself, but I will explain to him that it's tradition that we deal with it in our own ranks. He will believe that and be satisfied." "Good! Then that's settled. Problem detected, problem solved, I would say," The words flowed quickly from Francesco's mouth.

"Don't be so hasty, the problem still has to be dealt with. But tell me, dear Francesco, are you not interested to hear what happened? You have always been a loyal friend and have done your job without being curious. But this is a special situation and I could well imagine that curiosity is killing you."

Francesco replied without giving it a second thought,

108

"Boss, I know that you are always very careful and not talkative. Of course I would be interested in hearing the reasons. If you are going to tell me about it, then you will surely do so and if not, then it's not necessary."

Don Rosso looked into Francesco's eyes, "Those are true words that you have chosen there. I am not one to chit-chat and it is also not necessary for you to know the reason. I don't want to make problems in the first rank public. I hope you understand that. You know too well that I actually detest violence, but sometimes it can't be avoided. The address is Kampata 31, in the noble quarters of the University of Witwatersrand. But one more question! What happens to the bodyguards?"

Francesco replied softly, "I think that they will unfortunately have to suffer the same fate. As you already said, Eduardo always dines together with his bodyguards. It will be better if are also eliminated. It's common that unknown viruses are introduced there. Coincidences happen!"

Don Rosso said only very briefly, "Un dono del cielo! Not even those from the second rank will doubt this. Give me immediate feedback when the job is done. This doesn't suit me at all at the moment. I am busy with other important stuff. And please, no mistakes. We can't afford that at this time, otherwise we will spark a war in our own ranks." Don Rosso ended the conversation and said goodbye to Francesco.

Eduardo's fate was sealed. Although he had been a

high-ranking member of the closer family his entire life and grew up together and trustingly with everyone else, he always believed he was meant for better things. He would have rather preferred to take over Don Rosso's position. He was always so to say tipping the scales. Don Rosso had first of all believed that Eduardo wanted to negotiate a deal with the Italian police. But later it turned out that he planned to cooperate with the Russians.

Although Don Rosso got along with the Russian Mafia's top boss very well and they had become close friends over the years, the friendship ended at the competing borders. The boss of the Russian clan thought nothing about stopping on Don Rosso's doorstep.

After the Russian Mafia recognized Eduardo's weaknesses, the Russian boss set someone on him. He tried to win him and the organization behind him over, making of course great promises. Eduardo was to be the second man in the Russian clan.

That flattered him so much that he could not resist the offer and he got into closer and closer contact with the Russian Mafia. This could not happen unnoticed behind Don Rosso's back and soon he had learned about it from his informants, fortunately so early so that Eduardo had not put his plans into action yet and had not suspected he had been discovered already a long time ago.

Don Eduardo Rosso had sent Eduardo into the jungle in order to thwart his plans. Theoretically, the boss actually wanted to sort him out personally after the meeting. But the letter in which he learned that Eduardo had already arranged a personal meeting with the Russian Mafia boss had come beforehand, meaning that the matter had to be settled before the big family gathering. There was no way that Don Rosso wanted to wait until the turncoat presented a fait accompli because he was convinced that Eduardo was going to take 2nd and 3rd rank groups with him to the Russian Mafia. That way, a war would break out in their own ranks with an unpredictable result.

On the return flight to Palermo, Don Rosso let the entire conversation with Francesco go through his head once more. He felt relieved. He was happy about having solved a problem in such an elegant way once again. His good mood slowly returned and by the time he arrived back at his beloved villa, his anger was long disappeared.

Marian and her husband had been quite worried about the father and they were relieved to see a cheerful Don Rosso on the terrace the next morning. Everything was as always.

No, they didn't ask any questions. Her education told Marian that it was not the right time and Karl was still thinking about the letter opener that his angry father-in-law had slammed into the oak table.

Karl was never informed about the meaning of the incident. They never discussed it, not even later. Don Rosso held on to the saying: speech is silver, silence is gold.

On the terrace, Serjo stood up whistling and called out briefly, "Karl, come on," Then they walked over to the office. As soon as they sat together at the conference table, Karl said proudly, "I have the lists ready and I was up until late in the night putting together the hotels with suitable conference rooms. The best thing for us to do is take a suite in each of the hotels. You wanted a different location for each day of the conference. That means, also a different hotel. Is that right?"

Stunned by his assistant's enthusiasm for his work, Don Rosso replied, "Exactly. Perfect, my dear son-in-law. So let's start encrypting the invitations for the family members. Afterwards, the messages should be passed to the messengers via the lawyers ."

Don Rosso stood up and walked a few paces to the rear wall of the room where there was a safe. He opened it with a key and combination. Then he took out lists and said, "These are the encryption keys, they are only available on paper in the safe. Not on the computer. For safety reasons. Do you understand?"

The right hand was introduced to encryption technology

Don Rosso showed Karl the lists containing approximately 50 different encryption keys that had to be applied in the correct order. They started to encrypt each invitation with a different code. The code itself was in a letter in a separate envelope.

"This is the way it goes: The lawyer receives the invitation in an envelope and a separate envelope with the encryption key. He then gives each messenger the task of delivering the message to the address written on the envelope. One messenger brings the encrypted invitation, a different messenger the encryption key. Two completely different ways. Should a messenger become too curious, he will be unable to do anything with the contents even after opening the envelope as there is always one part missing. And after one unauthorized opening of an envelope, his wife would be unlikely to ever see him again.

Now you know how it all works. If we have very risky situations, additional envelopes are delivered using intermediate messengers. But that is not necessary this time as the information contained is not very meaningful."

Karl was amazed with how much effort and thought the family organized everything down to the last detail. On the same day, they finished the invitations and had them delivered to the lawyer by a chauffeur.

"Now we are done. Now we can takes things easy a bit. Are you going to fly to Paris with your wife the day after tomorrow?"

Karl replied, "That's our plan."

Don Rosso was satisfied, "Good, I can rest for a few days then. I desperately need it. Everything was a bit much lately, I have hardly had time to rest."

The Sunday lived up to its name. The sun shone and it was pleasantly mild as the couple left for the airport. The cloudless sky allowed for an endless view out of the airplane.

The city of love got to see a new director

Fortunately, the weather was no different in Paris either. After arriving at their hotel which was situated directly on the Avenue des Champs-Élysées, Marian invited Karl to go for a walk. "We should take a look at your new company domicile, I know exactly where it is." She quickly grabbed her short-sleeved jacket, took Karl's hand and dragged him out of the room. He followed without resistance as he was very curious about the company headquarters.

From the hotel it was no more than 800 meters to the Arc de Triomphe, which had been commissioned by Napoleon in 1806 as a sign of victory after the Battle of Austerlitz.

From there, a few steps away, you can reach a side street in which a well-preserved old building was located. The villa stood magnificently in a small park that was enclosed by medieval railings. The whole thing seemed very dignified and radiated a quiet serenity in the middle of the hectic Parisian traffic.

The gilded signboard with the inscription "La Finette AG, Medical Technic" that was mounted on the closed entry portal looked very respectable. Full of pride, Karl couldn't look at it all often enough. He walked around the park several times to have a closer look at everything.

Yes, these were his new company headquarters. He thought that even the executive of his former bank could become green with envy here. He would invite him to come. Or perhaps better not? Should not he like his father-in-law shine with more modesty?

Karl said to Marian in an extremely proud voice, "Magnificent, magnificent, It's hard to believe that I will be working here as a member of the board as of tomorrow. I could never have imagined in my wildest dreams that this would ever happen to me. My dearest, I owe this all to you. I couldn't imagine about what I might have missed if I hadn't sat down next to you on the park bench that day. I love you with all my heart."

Marian thought, then I would have been sitting there again the next Sunday. That had been the plan. But of course she didn't mention that. But at that precise moment she felt a bit like a liar.

"Let's go and eat, I'm starving now, I know a top restaurant," she said and pulled her beloved husband behind her.

The newlyweds strolled along the Champs-Élysées in the sunshine. The two bodyguards walked ahead of them fighting their way through the crowds.

They arrived at the restaurant that she and her father loved so much and sat down. As usual, they sat down at one table and the bodyguards at the next. No sooner had they sat down, a waiter appeared. He must have been new in the cafe, Marian had at least never seen him there before.

The waiter waved and called out loudly, "Madame, that's not a table for two, that's a table for four people."

One of the bodyguards immediately jumped to his feet, stood in front of the waiter and said, "Sorry, Madame is a very important person!" He pulled a 100 Euro note from his pocket and slipped it into the waiter's hand. The waiter expressed his thanks and continued in broken German, "Madame, please excuse the small misunderstanding. Of course, everything is all right. What may I serve you?"

Marian replied, "Le menu et deux verres de champagne, s'il vous plaît!" The menu and two glasses of champagne, Karl was satisfied with the choice.

The couple dined then undisturbed and enjoyed the close attention of the entire service staff. Marian told her husband, "I have a surprise for you. For tonight I have ordered a table for two in the Restaurant 58 on the Eiffel Tower. It is located on the first floor and has fantastic views over the city. This will be a romantic evening for the two of us. Well, what do you say?"
"Fantastic, you are the best and wisest wife that anybody could can imagine in the whole wide world," Karl replied enthusiastically.

After an afternoon nap in the hotel, they had the chauffeur show them the sights of the city

At 6 o'clock they arrived at the world famous Eiffel Tower. They took the elevator to the first floor. There, they chose a table with a wonderful view of the Paris sunset.

"A wonderful city. A fabulous experience. I am happy that I can share this view with the most beautiful and best wife in the world. Surely there cannot be anything more beautiful," These were Karl's enthusiastic words.

"I only can return that as a compliment to the best husband in the world. Look how magical Paris looks when the lights go on in the darkness. Look how well you can see the great cathedrals. There you can see Sacré-Coeur de Montmartre and there is the Notre Dame de Paris." Marian pointed to the respective buildings. Both were entranced by the magic of the city.

Karl could no longer hold himself in his chair. He stood up, hugged and kissed his wife. It couldn't have been more romantic. The couple radiated with happiness and it seemed as if nothing in the world could ever tarnish that happiness.
However, this was to change in the near future. It was a good thing that the happy couple were not aware of it that evening.

At about 10 o'clock the couple ended their romantic excursion and decided to continue the evening in their hotel suite.

The following morning, Karl, as the new board member, was driven to his company headquarters. A welcoming committee had organized a small reception for him. The directors of the company welcomed their new board member. Then he had the corporate balance sheets of the last three years brought to his new office by his attractive assistant.

He quickly gained an overview of the company. His equal board member colleague who managed the business operations of the company was a few years younger than Karl. Nevertheless, he had the company well under control. The company members spoke clear words in his favor.

Karl was delighted about the fact that there was no rivalry between the two board members. They worked together quite amicably. Karl had initially expected a small war with the existing head of the company. He was clever in that as new board member he had made it clear that he did not want to interfere in the operations of the company. That is why he only met cooperating employees.

He of course took lunch at a traditional café with his wife. Marian had brightened her day with a wellness program in the hotel and would continue this after eating together with her husband. Karl walked the few steps back to his office and continued with his balance sheet evaluations. As on the previous day, he was very satisfied with the numbers. And as there was no reason for complaints, he ended the audit impressed.

A storm caused the private jet to do a nose-dive

Early the next morning, the couple started out for the return flight to Palermo. The weather was a bit unsettled and cool.

The private jet was just approaching the Alps when severe turbulences arose. The machine was hit by a storm front and shaken violently.

When the aircraft captain asked the guests politely to fasten their seat belts, Karl took the hand of his fearful wife in order to calm her down a bit. The aircraft rocked violently in the swirling air masses.

The ups and downs of the plane made both of them feel sick, as a precaution they kept the sick bags that hat been provided handy.

The pilot apologized by announcement for the weather turbulences that could not be circumnavigated. Time and time again the aircraft plunged into emptiness as soon as it entered an air hole. The clouds formed a massive storm front. Lightning shot out of the rainy sky. The plane temporarily tipped over to one side and again there were cries of fear on board.

Nevertheless, the passengers trusted their experienced captain.

Then there was a brief announcement from the pilot again, "Dear passengers, the mistral wind is raging unexpectedly far into our flight path. I apologize for this again. We can assume that we will pass through the storm front shortly. Please remain seated and keep your seatbelts on. I will contact you as soon as there are any changes."

Don Rosso had been informed by phone by the flight engineer that the jet was flying through a heavy storm front and a delayed landing was to be expected.

He was worried about his daughter and Karl. He kept walking around the park like a tiger in a cage. As a precaution, he had canceled all business appointments for the next two days. Then he went into the house and turned on the television. In the news, a warning was being given about an uncommon storm.

"Damn it," he cried, "why did the captain ignore this warning?" Don Rosso grabbed the phone and called the airport, "Hello, air traffic control? Don Rosso here. Can you tell me some more details about the flight of my plane from Paris to Palermo?" His facial features darkened.

The flight security chief replied, "We do not have any more information except that a heavy storm front suddenly appeared after the machine had taken off. We have problems keeping in touch by radio with machines on this route. But as soon as we know any more detail, we will inform you immediately. Unfortunately, I must end the call now."

Don Rosso slammed the phone down and shouted out loudly, "It's unbelievable that with all today's technology, they are still unable to predict a storm. Those sleepyheads!"

The staff withdrew rather fearfully from the vicinity of their boss. A thunderstorm had not just opened on the flight route, but also in the Rosso villa. The Don was completely unnerved and poured himself a cognac at the bar in the living room sitting down on one of the chunky club chairs. Dark thoughts raced through his head.

The memory about his wife's early death arose within him. For a long time these had remained hidden. He remembered how his late wife had struggled against crucial pain in hospital for weeks and that the doctors hadn't known how to help her. After a long lingering illness, she was finally released from her misery. That had been a black period for Don Rosso who in addition also had to worry about his frightened child. He would not be able to survive such a test again.

The aircraft continued to be spun around by the storms like a plaything of the air. Suddenly the machine dropped to a lower altitude. After a few hundred meters, the captain was able to hold the machine again and go into a climb. For Marian, there was no holding back now. She held the sick bag to her mouth and vomited violently. Worried, Karl looked at his beloved wife.

Some time passed that seemed like an eternity to the couple and the crew. Again and again, the jet descended in the direction of the earth and could in be held again. Then a further announcement came from the cockpit, "Some of the on-board electronics have failed. Even though we have the machine largely under control, please prepare yourself for an unplanned emergency landing."

Karl and Marian were dumb with shock. Even the stewardess was no longer herself and had become as white as a sheet. The minutes passed and seemed like hours. During those moments no one dared to say even a word. The silence in the machine was only interrupted by the loud roar of the thunder. Fear spread throughout the machine. Would they make it to the next airport?

"We have identified a nearby sports airport and will begin with the emergency landing in a few moments. Prepare yourself for a hard landing," the captain informed.

The stewardess distributed extra pillows and frantically checked the guests' seatbelts. "Lay your faces on the pillow between your legs," she said curtly returning to her seat again to fasten her own belt.
Meanwhile, Don Rosso had spoken with the head of security at the airport again. He had received a radio message that the jet was trying to reach an alternative airport in the area. He wanted to inform Don Rosso as soon as there were any new messages. "I want to be called on the spot! As soon as you hear something! After all, I am not just anyone and my daughter is not a charter passenger. If you want to keep your job a while longer, then you had better act accordingly," cried Don Rosso down the phone and would not be calmed down. He slammed the receiver down again

and rampaged through the house. Now he had finally lost his composure. He had never smashed bottles or anything else in his whole life, but now he threw glasses and bottles around the room in order to blow off a bit of steam.

The butler feared for his life and raced out of the room. Once again Don Rosso drank a cognac, but the more he drank, the more he got out of control. Nothing could keep him calm. "Bring me my daughter back or somebody will die." echoed through the villa. Countless jars and bottles shattered with a loud crash against the walls.

With a cracking sound, the jet hit the runway and was hurled back and forth by the upwinds. Just as they finally seemed to have found solid ground, the machine sped towards the end of the runway. Those present prayed desperately that the jet would come to a full stop in time. The markings at the end of the landing strip came closer and closer. What would be at the end of the markings? Maybe a steep slope? The few seconds that were full of questions seemed like days to the couple.

"There! We've come to a standstill! We've made it. We are saved." Karl fell into the arms of his terror-stricken wife. The flight attendant and crew also embraced each other relieved. Some time passed until the visibly exhausted captain asked if anything had happened to anybody. Apart from a few scratches, everybody had survived the landing.

"Thank God everything went well! Madame, I've never experienced anything like that in my whole career. The wonderful captain has saved all of our lives," said the first officer and shook the captain's hands gratefully. "It was worse than we first thought," admitted the captain and added softly. "The runway is suitable for good weather aircraft but not for jets like ours."

Don Rosso jumped to the phone, the airport boss was on the line, "They landed safely. Nobody has been hurt. Don Rosso, I am pleased to tell you that they landed safely in Sargente at a small sport airport and everything is fine. I hope they are all doing well. The message reached me just one minute ago. I must get back to work, I hope you understand and are no longer angry with me?"

"Mamma mia, God be praised, all are well. My Marian and Karl, they are all in good shape. Thank you! Thank you my dear. I owe you a favor and excuse my lapse earlier on. I deeply apologize and ask for your understanding." He plopped into the club chair. "I can't describe how happy I am." "That's fine, I understand," the head of security ended the conversation.

"My mobile phone! Where is my mobile phone?" The slightly drunken boss' voice echoed throughout the villa, he was overjoyed and all smiles. The butler came running towards him and gave him his mobile phone. Slightly tipsy Don Rosso dialed Marian's phone number. He heard the ring tone on the line, but no one answered the call. Then he heard a soft voice, "Hi Daddy, everything is find. Apart from being frightened, nothing happened to either Karl or me.

There is a big commotion here at the moment, I'll get back to you later."

Don Rosso was overjoyed, "I can't tell you how happy I am about the fact that you are safe. I was in deadly fear and in a state of near despair. Yes, call me again later."

The inhabitants of the small town Sargente had all gathered at the sports airport. The inhabitants of the idyllic little city didn't want miss the adventure. The policemen and firemen accompanied the crew members of the aircraft and the passengers to the small and inconspicuous airport building. The very low lighting in the small airport made everything look even eerier to the rescued group .

As they reached the building, they were surrounded by press who were taking photos with their cameras for all it was worth. Everybody was in a state of great excitement and happy about the rescue.

Finally after a precautionary medical examination and a brief questioning by the police Marian and Karl were released. They were allowed to be driven to a nearby hotel. The rooms of the small and inconspicuous hotel were equipped with only the most necessary things, but that didn't bother anyone now. Their needs were restricted to shower and sleep. Maybe this would help them to lose the inner tension that still existed.

After an hour, which seemed to Don Rosso like an eternity in his excitement, he called the butler, "Put me through to the airport in Sargente."

The servant dialed the phone number of information frantically, "Good day, I need the phone number of the sports airport in Sargente or can you put me straight through now?" "I can connect, please wait a moment." the information desk connected and the butler heard: "Airport Central in Sargente, good day."

"Residence of the Rosso family in Palermo, good day. Don Rosso would like to be put through to a responsible person from your house who can give him information about the emergency landing. He is the father of one of the passengers,"

"Listen, you are now surely the hundredth caller from the press posing as a relative. I can't put you through. But if you really are a relative, you can give me your phone number and we will call you back," the lady replied in a friendly tone.

Don Rosso had listened to the conversation on the loudspeaker and snatched up the phone furiously, "You listen, I am the father of Marian Rosso and also the owner of the MacDonnell Douglas, and if a responsible person of your small airport doesn't call me back in the next five minutes , you can earn your money by lugging banana boxes for the next days. You can see my phone number."

"You cannot believe how many calls I have received today and anyway, how are you speaking to me? I have already copied your telephone number from the display and will pass this on to the airport manager now. Should he consider it necessary, he will call you back shortly. I wish you a nice day." At the same time, the lady in the call center slammed down the receiver.

Don Rosso barely had time to get upset. When the phone rang again, he immediately picked up the receiver.

"Good day, Don Rosso, my name is Lamberto Dini, I am the airport manager. I apologize but since your machine made an emergency landing here, all hell has broken loose. As a small airport, we were not prepared for something like this. What can I do for you?" Don Rosso was reconciled a bit and said, "Mr. Dini, I wanted to ask about my daughter, I can't reach her by phone." The airport manager assured him, " Thanks to the excellent captain and apart from a shock, nothing happened to either your daughter nor the other passengers. We have accommodated the passengers in a small hotel so that they can recover a bit from the excitement. I know that the cell phone reception there is very bad, I will give you the phone number of the hotel."

"Good," Don Rosso replied and wrote down the number of the hotel. "And thank you for your understanding, please excuse my exceptional behavior."

In the meantime, Don Rosso had taken a look at a map in order to make out the exact location of Sargente. The city was too far away to drive there quickly. So he had no choice but to wait and patience was not one of his best traits. Nervously, Don Rosso dialed the phone number of the hotel and asked for the hotel owner. It was more likely a simple inn. The worried father asked how the couple was doing. The hotel manager informed him awed and willingly that they had withdrawn to their room and were probably now resting.

Don Rosso also wanted to calm his nerves now with a bit of sleep and retired to his bedroom, but not without telling his butler that he should inform him immediately if there was any news. He slept through soundly until the next day. When he got up he was well rested.

No sooner than Serjo taken his place at the breakfast table, he heard his cell phone ringing. "Hi Dad, Marian here. We are fine again. It was terrible, you cannot imagine how frightened we were. But now everything is all right again. I have just spoken to the aircraft captain. He has recommended that we go to Bologna by car and take a scheduled flight to Palermo. He thinks the runway in Sargente could be too short and he might have problems getting the machine started properly. The on-board electronics also have to be repaired. There is nothing extensive that has to be repaired but it will take a time. Therefore, Karl and I have decided that we will come with the next scheduled flight." Her father thought about that and answered, " Yes, that will probably be for the best. I'm glad that everything ended well. I'm sitting here as if on tenterhooks. Come home quickly, so that we can recover from the experience together."

Two hours after the phone call, the couple had already ordered a taxi and drove to Bologna airport. They booked first class seats of a respectable airline that took off in the direction of Palermo a short time later. Although the loving couple still didn't feel really comfortable after their last experience with flying, they were already looking forward to being back at home soon. This reduced the fear of flying a bit.

After a gentle landing on the runway at Palermo, Marian rushed into the waiting room to her father and fell into his arms. Then Don Rosso also hugged his son-in-law. They were overjoyed that they were together again and the welcome took more than half an hour.

As ordered by his boss, the chauffeur had bought a particularly beautiful bouquet of flowers for the daughter that was so big, she could hide her face behind it. The press had also somehow found out about the arrival of the couple. The airport exit was teeming with photographers. The Rosso bodyguards had their hands full to push back the crowds of journalists in order to form a lane to the car for the boss and his entourage. "What a pantomime! Is there no way of stemming the sensation-greedy press ?" Don Rosso's pithy voice sounded angry.

When they arrived at the villa Rosso totally nerve-wracked, the villa was besieged by insatiable paparazzi and the guards had great difficulty keeping the masses off the private property. After the limousine had entered the gates, the guards pushed back the crowd until the gates had closed. It was extremely unpleasant for the boss to be so present in public now. He shrank away from public appearances or interviews for good reason.

A welcoming committee of staff stood at the entrance of the villa excited and happy about the return of the couple. They welcomed Marian and her Karl warmly as if they themselves had escaped death and were now returning. Don Rosso held a loud speech so that all could hear , "Let them arrive in peace first. Tomorrow is another day and then they can tell us everything." Then he turned to the couple, "I presume you want to recover a bit in your room first?" Karl said, "You are absolutely right. We have to recover from the experience first and I think a few hours of rest would be appropriate for us. " They withdrew to their bedroom. The domestic staff returned to their work chatting.

As a precaution, Don Rosso had arranged for a psychologist to examine the couple and help them to get over the experience.

Next morning, after his first coffee, he went to his office alone and opened the mail. Then he decrypted the messages as usual. Francesco had sent him information that he read greedily. Everything had gone well. There had been no problems in dealing with the job in Africa. Francesco had carried out the plan successfully. At least that had worked out without incident. Now Don Rosso had to inform the boss in Hong Kong quickly so that the Chinese would at long last end their search for the killer. Now of all times his private plane was damaged, how annoying. As if he had nothing else to do.

The time for the planning of the important family meeting was running out. He still had to plan how to explain everything to the boys. With "boys", he meant the bosses of the first rank.

In Hong Kong, the Mafia boss met the boss of the Triad clan

It was no good, he had to go and see the Asian boss of the Triads personally. A message or a phone call in such an important matter wasn't appropriate and too dangerous. It was important to keep up appearances that he was taking the matter very seriously and did not want to offend the Asian boss. The matter had to be dispensed with once and for all.

He had first-class seats booked for the next day already on a direct flight to Hong Kong for himself and his bodyguards and sent a message to the Asian boss. He asked the Triad boss for an urgent personal meeting during the night of the day after next. He had planned his return flight for three days later. He wanted to return to his daughter again as quickly as possible.

Directly after her therapy session, he told Marian the bad news that he had to travel urgently to Asia.

Karl spent his time with Marian playing tennis and lost one game after the other. Afterwards he enjoyed a pleasant cooling in the pool. He got over the emergency landing much faster than his wife. He would have liked to continue with his work already after two days. Some time ago Don Rosso had arranged for him to have his own access authorization to the conference room so he could now enter the work area independent of his father-in-law.

However, for his wife's sake, he waited a little while

longer.

After three days, he couldn't stand it any longer. He went to his desk and began to enter into the database the communication on the company's investments that the trustees had sent him.

While completing the current situation in his database, new query options kept popping up in his head that he expanded continuously. Thanks to the data now collected, he was quickly in a position to address all possible questions in a meaningful way.

According to the communications that Karl had received, the companies in which they had their investments were already busy with the installation of the management software. Everything was running to plan and the Don would certainly be very satisfied with the result.

Don Rosso and his men reached the metropolis of Hong Kong. He was very impressed with the hustle and bustle of the busy Chinese.

If you want to buy something cheap, then Hong Kong is the best place to do it. You can get just about everything you could imagine in this city. Original or an inexpensive copies of brands can be purchased there day and night. The shops are all open 24 hours a day and customers never need to worry about closing times.

But Don Rosso was not in a shopping mood now. After getting little sleep during the overnight flight, he wanted to reach the hotel quickly in order to overcome the jet lag.

Asians take special care of their guests. Hence, the Hong Kong hosts had arranged for some of the employees to act as considerate guides for Don Rosso. These picked the boss from Europe up at the airport with a vehicle convoy and brought him to his hotel. The meeting of the bosses was planned in a Chinese restaurant for the next day already.

The next evening, the Chinese drove Don Rosso to the harbor by luxury limousine so that he could cross over to a ship restaurant by speed boat.

When the passengers arrived, the heavily guarded boat restaurant was brightly illuminated. The view over the night-time silhouette of Hong Kong had impressed Don Rosso so much that his tension seemed to have disappeared during the crossing. This was not the first time he was seeing this amazing city at night. However, from the sea, it was always a grandiose sight that enchanted him time and time again.

There had till now been no opportunity to show this spectacle to his daughter. Marian had already traveled far, but Asia was a place she had never been to before. While Don Rosso was thinking about showing his daughter Hong Kong soon, they arrived at the restaurant and were led up the gangway. The boat was decorated splendidly in Asian style and moved gently on the sea waves. Light classical dance music filled the otherwise quiet deck.

A Chinese man asked Don Rosso in English to enter the restaurant room. Before accepting the request, he glanced around briefly taking a closer look at the night-time shore of the city. Then he entered the dining room politely taking off his sunglasses and his black hat. He had chosen this paraphernalia for when he was in the hotel so that could protect himself from prying eyes and hide his face.

"Good day and welcome. We have indeed not seen each other for several years," the Chinese boss spoke in the finest English. "I am really happy to see my great friend and colleague personally again after such a long time. As you know, my dear Don Rosso, I admire you very much and I am happy to welcome you here today as my guest."

They both then sat down at a large round table.

Don Rosso replied, "I am also delighted to see my longtime business partner again after such a long time and to see that he is in good health. The honor is all mine. Thank you very much for your great hospitality, Mister Leeyoung. You haven't aged a bit since I saw you the last time if you allow me this comment."

Gracefully Leeyoung spoke, "Let us eat together. According to Asian tradition, you can talk business better during a good meal. "

He clapped his hands and the staff immediately brought vast amounts of different dishes. In the middle of the table there was a turntable so you could easily pass the separate dishes to your table partner.

The huge variety of dishes assured that you were spoiled for choice. Everything of course had to be sampled. At the same time, a still mineral water was served.

When all the dishes had been served, the Asian boss clapped his hands twice and the staff disappeared out of the room. Now the two of them were alone together and could start their private conversation.

"I hope you like it, my very dear Don Rosso. Unfortunately, the chefs here are not used to preparing food according to the European taste." But this was more just a polite formality from the Chinese man.

"This seafood is excellent. I like Asian food a lot," Serjo Rosso replied.

With relish they tried all the different dishes that had been served. Wise Don Rosso was familiar with the Asian table culture that did not allow him to be the first to start a business conversation. That was reserved for the host. Out of courtesy, Mister Leeyoung normally let some time pass before he started asking how business was going. A polite gesture that Leeyoung had taken over from the Japanese was that there would be no "no" for him towards a guest. A rejection would be strictly skated around and a stubborn follow-up from Europeans was frowned upon. But this was nothing new to the well-traveled Don Rosso.

He began, "Well, we are actually quite satisfied with the way our business is progressing. The Indians are now trying to gain a foothold in our areas. But as long as we and our families stick together, they will not really have a chance to push us out," For negotiating-related reasons, he added straight away, "Our family has absolutely no intention of expanding or challenging other ancestral territories."

Mister Leeyoung looked over to Don Rosso interested and said, "That's right, as long as we stick together, nobody can push us out. You are a wise man, Don Rosso. I think the market is large enough for all of us."

This particular show of friendliness was without great significance. Don Rosso knew this. Even if they parted as best friends, this would still not rule out the possibility that one of the Chinese would shoot him from behind the next hedge.

Don Rosso began purposefully, "Dear Mister Leeyoung, I have come to thank you personally for the good cooperation over the past years. At the same time, I want to apologize for a regrettable misdemeanor of a family member. My whole family kindly asks for your generous indulgence and forgiveness."

The Chinese listened attentively without interrupting the Italian boss. He even paused eating for a short time as he was so tense. It would have been rude to interrupt or question what he was saying so he waited patiently until his dialog partner gave him more details.

"As I said, a closer family member has made a faux pass for unknown reasons and personally killed one of your bosses in Bangkok. Neither the family members nor I were informed in advance about this. He fired the shot completely without authorization. My entire family had no way of preventing this. We deeply regret what happened and grieve with you."

Mister Leeyoung spoke slowly and with careful consideration, "This is very unfortunate. Are you sure you still have everything under control, my dear friend? I have to tell you that we were very upset about the incident. I must confess to the shame of my family that we checked all the clans and searched for the culprit everywhere but without success. Only your members have not yet been subject to close scrutiny. However, this was already planned and was to be carried out in the near future. Therefore it's good that you have come to visit me at exactly the right time. If you tell me who the culprit is, we are sure to avoid unnecessary bloodshed."

After his announcement, Mister Leeyoung continued eating, visibly satisfied. He was not particularly excited, but you could clearly feel the gravity of the situation in the air.

For Don Rosso it was clear that the Chinese clan was plotting revenge. This could not go unpunished. In the eyes of the Chinese it was loss of face if the culprit didn't receive his deserved punishment and they would not be satisfied until this deed had been avenged.

He continued explaining, "Mister Leeyoung, with all due respect, surely you have had a situation where you had to accept a faux pas in your family. Nobody knows what disputes have taken place between your and our members. When I became aware of this unbelievable conspiracy, we also began searching in order to assist our Asian friends in their grief. We also of course checked our own ranks. Soon we came across our family member Eduardo, from our inner circle." After the name had been mentioned, the tension increased in the room.

"My dear Don Rosso, I am very pleased and honored that you are speaking to me so frankly. You have convinced me that you still have your clan under control and are the undisputed boss. Unfortunately, the matter is not done with yet. Our rule is, ne of us for three of the others. That is our culture. I beg your understanding."

The conversation had become harder and despite all the niceties, the parties' positions were clear and couldn't be questioned. Don Rosso had already expected that a simple apology would not be enough to calm the Asians down.

Now he introduced his second ace. "Of course I understand your qualified concerns, my dear Mrs. Leeyoung. If he hadn't stemmed from our inner family circle, it would also have not been a problem to hand the culprit over to you. We brought the culprit to justice so that we avoid all difficulties and in order to bring peace to your and our family and members. Our family tradition only allows us to be the ones who punish close family members. Eduardo was poisoned by us and died in agony." Don hoped that these words would soothe his table companion.

Leeyoung continued, "It is excellent that you acted so selflessly, dear Don Rosso, our family will surely bear you no grudge. However, my very generous friend Rosso, we certainly cannot satisfy my family with only one sacrifice. The wife and the children usually have to suffer for this as well."

Serjo had also expected this and now he was trying to get the best out of the negotiations. Hoping to protect Eduardo's innocent wife and children against a retaliation campaign, he gave exact thought as to how he could continue the difficult negotiations.

"Honored Leeyoung, as a wise boss of your organization you are as interested as we are that we continue our business as peacefully as possible. Neither you nor I are keen to be disturbed in our undertakings through family feuds. Although I understand and accept your culture, as leaders we both need to make clear to our clans that with the death of the culprit, the matter been brought to a final end. I am sure that my family members will not tolerate further sacrifices. Therefore, I vouch with my own life that something like this will never be repeated again. I ask you very kindly to talk to your family and persuade them to not cause Eduardo's relatives any further anguish."

The polite Leeyoung replied, "I am very happy that we can discuss this unpleasant thing in private here. It is good that you have found your way to me quickly and that you look at the situation with the necessary seriousness of the situation. You demand quite a lot from your old friend, but that you know yourself already. I personally accept both your apology and also with a heavy heart that you have settled the matter yourself. To cut a long story short my friend, I will talk to my people and tell them that the regrettable matter has been finally settled here and now. So that our family friendship can look forward to an unclouded shared future."

Don Rosso was happy, "I am very relieved and very grateful to the generous Mister Leeyoung. Let us drink a toast to our new great friendship and the solidarity of our families that in future will be infinite. To your health!"

Leeyoung also raised his glass and said, "To your health. Today let us celebrate the new agreement together. For tomorrow, I have organized a sightseeing tour of the city for you."

Serjo replied, "Thank you very much for the very generous hospitality. Without wanting to be rude, as a father of a daughter I ask for your leniency. Two days ago, my daughter survived an emergency landing of her plane and she is still quite weak. Therefore I would prefer, dear Mister Leeyoung, to leave tomorrow. You too have children yourself and I imagine you can understand my personal concerns."

The Chinese boss replied, "I understand that very well, you have my full sympathy. And all the more I appreciate that you have come to see me for this meeting, despite your personal problems. Of course you must fly back to your dear daughter tomorrow. This is a friendly order, but now we will celebrate."

He rang a bell, a band played and a group of Chinese dancers performed folk dances. The evening lasted until late into the night and after a hearty good-bye Don Rosso was taken back to his hotel.

Once in his hotel room, he immediately went to bed. He let the day's events go through his mind for a few minutes more and was satisfied with the results. Then his eyes closed.

The next day, he was driven to the airport without breakfast and caught his flight back to Palermo. He wanted to be back with his daughter as quickly as possible.

In the villa, the newlyweds had heard nothing about the father's difficult negotiations and continued with their daily activities as usual. Barely had Don Rosso appeared in the park again, Marian called, "Daddy, daddy, I am so happy. Karl, daddy is back!"

Still completely exhausted her father greeted her, "My dears, I am so happy that you are pleased to see me , but first of all I must get some rest from the long trip. As soon as I am fit again, I will join you." Then Serjo disappeared into his bedroom. After the long-haul flight and the difficult past few days, he was dead on his feet. One could see that he had had a few exhausting days behind him.

Karl said to Marian, "Yes, let him get his breath back first. He is as young as he used to be and a long journey like that demands its price. In the meantime, don't you want to lose a tennis game at long last?"

143

Everyday life returned to normal for a short time

"Christmas will never come early? You will never win against me. Even if I find it a shame for my dear husband, I still won't do him this favor." And off she ran in the direction of the tennis court. "Game, set and match. You didn't manage again," her scream of joy echoed across the tennis court. In reality, Karl's mood after the game was contained. Should the rules of game maybe be changed?

Don Rosso only appeared briefly for dinner and then disappeared again to continue resting in bed. Only very little was said at the table out of consideration for him.

Even before Marian had ended her beauty sleep the next morning, Karl was up and about sitting at his workplace. He has nearly finished his database and had already entered all the information. The response of lawyers in Palermo that hotels and flights for the family member meeting had been successfully booked had also arrived.

Only two more months were left till the big event. Don Rosso also wanted to use the meeting to introduce Karl to the participants as his right hand. Karl was waiting for that just as eagerly as for the announcement of the grand plan for the future.

Karl was working in the conference area when his father-in-law showed up unexpectedly. "Hi Karl," he said still a bit tired, "I just wanted to check on the mail. Is there anything new?"

"I had not expected you back at work so quickly," Karl answered and reported on the good news. "Everything is going fine here so far. The hotels for the meeting and the flights are booked. My database for the company's holdings is finished except for a few more steps and the first companies have placed their orders for the management software. I think we will be able to access a few companies in a few weeks already."

He continued explaining, "Oh yes, we have not had a chance to talk about my stay in Paris and my audit at La Finette. The company is solid and I am getting on really well with my fellow board member. All in all, everything is running well there. There is a good atmosphere amongst the employees, the balance sheets are correct. What more is there to say? No complaints."

"That's good," Don Rosso said, "It really is a fine company with a great future. Write to your fellow board member that we will hold a general meeting on the 23rd of July with the supervisory board and the shareholders including you, and that I have asked you to invite the shareholders and supervisory board members. And of course everything in a very friendly form. In addition, inform him that he does not need to be present personally at the meeting and that we are only discussing a possible expansion of the company. Then he as board member has no reason to worry. Karl, thanks for your help, I don't know what I would do without you."

145

Then he sat down at his desk and wrote two messages which he then encrypted. These he then handed them over to a chauffeur for delivery to his lawyer. The first message was for Francesco, the killer: *Hello Francesco, meeting in 3 days at meeting point Nr. 4 at the usual time. Trip to Hong Kong was successful.* The second message was for Antonio, who was responsible for the European market: *Urgent business meeting in my villa in four days.*

After completion, Don Rosso asked his son-in-law, "Would you like us to eat lunch together at Pedro's at the harbor tomorrow? I'm off again. I'll have a swim in the pool for a while and then read the newspapers. See you." As he left, he heard Karl's agreement, "Yes, of course, it makes my mouth water when I think of that wonderful fish platter. Marian will also for sure be happy."

When he was away, Serjo had kept all the newspapers for Don Rosso so that he could go through them later. He browsed through them and noticed that the plane crash had been reported about in detail. One newspaper even included a report about him. He was, of course, presented as being a successful and impeccable businessman. Nevertheless, he felt slightly ill at ease because he didn't want to be too well known in the press. Who knew whether that would maybe tempt a curious press reporter to try and find out more about the successful person Rosso.
Afterwards, he put the papers aside and watched some television to relax until he fell asleep. When he woke up it was already late in the evening.

146

The following morning, before the three of them went to the harbor to Pedro's restaurant, Don Rosso wrote a long letter of condolence to Eduardo's wife. He expressed his deep shock that her husband had died because of an unknown virus and cancelled his attendance at the funeral for health reasons. In addition, he assured her that she would still receive financial support from the company investments. It would, of course, not have been a problem for him to attend the funeral in Palermo, but it would have too unpleasant for him to look the relatives in the eyes.

"My friends," echoed Pedro's voice through the bustling restaurant, "you are here again at last." He led them to a table on the terrace with the nicest view over the harbor. He pulled out a chair and pointed to it politely. Then he whirled his towel around a bit on the seat as if to remove nonexistent crumbs." Madame Rosso, my dear Marian, please. Don Rosso, my dear Serjo, and son-in-law, Karl, welcome." It obviously gave him great pleasure to perform this ceremony. But he actually practiced this spectacle for every guest who visited his restaurant more than twice. When Don Rosso came, he exaggerated it even more and it wouldn't have taken much and he would have kneeled down.

Then the restaurant owner started singing the famous song "O sole mio" receiving thunderous applause from the audience.

After the excellent meal, the Rossos ended the day with a stroll along the harbor promenade.

Next day, Karl asked his father-in-law in the conference room how fast the news had reached their destination. The Don told him that this was done in a flash as the messengers took direct flights to deliver the messages to their destinations. But that wasn't enough for Karl. He wanted to know how very urgent matters, that couldn't be delayed, were dealt with.

Don Rosso explained this as follows, "In particularly urgent cases the lawyer is asked to call the subject and ask him to call back. The subject calls back from a pay phone and receives the encrypted message by phone. The code that the subject received with the last written notification also applies for this oral message." Karl found this very clever, because nobody had to agree first which code should be used. "Don Rosso, do you play tennis too?" His son-in-law asked a hypocritical question. He had hoped that he might have the chance of at least winning this way. Puzzled Don Rosso stared at him and replied, "Of course I play tennis. But do you really think that you can win against me?"

"I just thought that you might like to play." Karl noticed that he had been caught out. In order to change the subject quickly, he threw in, "The private jet is ready for takeoff again at the hangar in Palermo. They called while you were in Hong Kong. It was only something minor in the on-board electronics that was damaged. I think once my wife is finished with the psychologist, I'll drive with her to the beach and have a picnic, is that okay with you?"

Serjo replied, "That's a very good idea, but let me now continue working here, I still have a lot to do."

While the boss made preparations for the discussions during the next few days, the couple spent a beautiful day on the beach. They had already recovered from the experience of the emergency landing and didn't think about it any longer. The paparazzi had also already left in order to devote their time to other things.

The killer was happy that the move in Hong Kong had worked

Before the couple got up the next morning, Don Rosso was already sitting in the car on his way to meeting point No. 4. When he got there, his special friend had not yet arrived. He had to wait, worried, one whole hour for Francesco. "I apologize but my flight was delayed. Today of all days. I am very sorry, boss." Conscience-stricken, Francesco took Don Rosso's right hand to kiss it.

Don Rosso replied, "Just don't make a habit it. Or do you also want to deprive me of power?" He smiled forgivingly. "Of course not, boss! I took the first machine and it had to make an non-scheduled stopover in Munich. We arrived in Palermo two hours late." The boss replied sullenly, "Non-scheduled stopovers are slowly becoming a habit. Now tell me, how did everything go in Africa?" "Everything was fine, no problem at all. They had ordered their favorite food which I simply spiced up. And after everyone started digging into it, the show started. They didn't even have time to call an ambulance. The cleaning lady found the bodies the next day. And that was it. And how was Hong Kong?"

Don Rosso began slowly, "That wasn't as easy as it was for you. The Chinese boss made a fuss for a long time and I had to keep going down on my knee. But then he relented in a spirit of friendship. Imagine, he could hardly be dissuaded from letting the wife and children also suffer. We talked together half the night and first I thought I wouldn't be able to convince him to leave Eduardo's relatives alone. After toing and froing, I was finally able to convince him that something like that will not happen again. The matter is definitely settled now." Francesco was delighted, " Boss, you are and remain the greatest of all. You are the smartest and best. I couldn't imagine a better boss. Now we can all sleep well again. Thank you, thank you so much."

"That's okay," Serjo Rosso said. "Take some vacation now. Take off to your island and if I need you, I'll call you." "I'll do that, boss and all the best. Thanks again and see you soon." Then Francesco rushed away.

Don Rosso arrived back at the villa and heard the couple romping about in the pool. "It's like a kindergarten here," he called out to the two. "Hi Daddy," Marian waved back. "We have to do this, the loser has to cool off." Karl spoke gruffly, "I have still a name or do I now have to change my first name in my passport into 'loser'?" Don Rosso said briefly, "Has he lost at tennis again? Maybe you should slowly give that up, otherwise we'll have a divorce in the family." Everybody, apart from poor Karl, was having a wonderful time.

"Loser, shall we meet in the conference room in one hour for a meeting?" Don Rosso asked grinning. Karl replied, "All right. Karl Rosso will be there. But before that, I have to discipline my wife."

The agenda for the international meeting of the bosses was set up

Don Rosso entered the conference room where the so-called loser was already waiting for him, enthusiastic to get to work. He began, "Let's discuss the planning for the big family reunion in detail once again. This is how I imagine it will be: July 20th – a Sunday – is the day everyone arrives. On July 23rd we start the meeting. Until then they can relax. Oh yes, we also need something like an agenda, can you take care of that?"

"Sure, no problem. If you tell me the facts briefly I will arrange everything today or tomorrow," Karl replied.

"So we start on the 23rd which is a Wednesday at 11 a.m.. That should be enough time for everyone to arrive easily. First item on the agenda is a short speech from me with a minute of silence for our deceased Eduardo. Afterwards we will continue with a brief presentation of your person. Then we will receive a report from the individual members on the current situation of the nine family members and there will also be a general exchange."

Karl asked, "I thought there are ten members?" Don Rosso continued, "Please, do not interrupt me! Unfortunately, one recently left us. Let's continue. The individual reports and the exchange will probably fill July 23rd. When we are in the new hotel the next day, I will explain reorganization. On Friday, July 25th, I will grant each member a personal interview of approximately one hour."

"On Saturday we will do a boat trip on the Rhine together with the spouses followed by a joint meal and dancing in the ballroom. Sunday is at the free disposal of everyone. On the Monday morning an exchange of the member's views will take place as well as the voting of the members on the reorganization. We will schedule the Tuesday for unexpected matters, and, if necessary, additional personal meetings. On Tuesday evening we end the meeting with a men's evening only. Wednesday, July 30th is general departure day for everybody. By that time I will be ready for a vacation. Everything okay, my dear fellow, or was that too fast for you?"

"True to scale, planned like a military attack. Everything is fine, my dear father-in-law. Then I will take care of the boat tour, the ballroom and the men's evening. I understand what you mean with men's evening. I will write the agenda tomorrow, is that okay?" The former Mr. Grosser grinned and continued, "But I still have one question. Why a vote? You are the boss who makes all the decisions!"

"But for a change of this dimension, I would like a vote as an exception. So that the whole thing is backed by everyone," Don Rosso said. "I understand boss."

"Perfect, we are a dream team. Now then, off into the sun with you! Tomorrow I have external appointments again." "Yes, off to the renegade wife," Karl cried.

Both now treated each other with humor and laughed together even though the boss had indicated at the beginning that there would be no fun in the conference room.

There Don Rosso thought like Konrad Adenauer: Everything changes and why should I care about the rubbish I said yesterday?

The European boss also took over leadership in Italy

When Antonio, a family member of the first rank and responsible for the European market, drove up to the villa the next day, he was greeted hospitably by Don Rosso. He led Antonio to a guest room and, after a short refreshment, he was asked to come out onto the terrace.

The Don was sitting there with a cup of coffee reading the newspaper when Antonio sat down next to him.

He began, "Come on, tell me Antonio, how are your wife and children doing?"

After a hand kiss Antonio told him, " Everything is fine so far. Well, sometimes I argue with my wife, but where does that not happen? The children are growing splendidly. The smallest one is such a sweet little mouse. But you'll see her when we get together at the big meeting. There was one other thing, I wanted to apologize that I couldn't come to Marian's wedding. That damned flu knocked me out for a few days. I hope you accept my sincere apologies."

Don Rosso stood up and replied, "Yes, that's fine, we know that this was not just an excuse. But come on, I want to introduce you personally to Karl."
They went down to the basement of the villa to the conference room.

"Hello my dear son-in-law, already working hard? I want to introduce you to Antonio, I have already told you about him. He is responsible for our markets in Europe. Antonio, this is Karl, Marian's husband who become my right hand a few weeks ago. We work really well together and Karl is a smart guy. Only playing tennis hasn't gone that well yet."

Antonio and Karl shook hands and greeted each other warmly.

Don Rosso added, "If you are done with the exchange of pleasantries, Antonio and I can start to work. Karl, would you leave the conference room and continue working at your desk so that I can have a private conversation with Antonio, please? Thank you for your understanding."

The visitor and the boss had barely taken their seats when Antonio started, "Your son-in-law is your right hand? Are you sure? Is that not a risk?"

Don Rosso stood by his decision, "He is already by vow committed to the family. We had him checked out beforehand. For months. I urgently needed support and he is proving himself extremely well. Don't worry, he is absolutely perfect and knows everything already."

"Well, then let's hope you are right, boss," Antonio replied. " We never have taken such a risk before. But I'm sure you know what you are doing. Why have you actually summoned me here?"

"Yes, let's get down to business. Have you heard about Eduardo's terrible fate?" Don Rosso looked at him questioningly.

"Nothing in detail, what happened?", the European boss wanted to know.

"A virus infection in Africa, all of a sudden, completely mystifying, but unfortunately it happened," Don Rosso said.

"Is it absolutely certain that our competitors are not behind it? Who takes over his job now?" Antonio wanted to know.

"There is no doubt, we have already checked everything possible," the Don confirmed. "But I'm sure you remember that we had no proper place for this fool in our ranks. That we organized the position extra for him. His position will not be occupied anymore. You will take over the tasks. It even fits quite well as regards organization."

Antonio felt honored and was happy that Italy had finally also been added to his area of activity now.

"Yes, that suits me well. It belongs to the European activities. It was always a thorn in my side anyway. Thank you for your confidence." Antonio stood up, knelt down before Don Rosso and kissed his hand. Then he asked the question, "How will I be introduced as boss in the 2nd and 3rd ranks?"

"Don't worry," the boss said. "I have it all planned. The day after tomorrow you will meet together with the second rank clan. I have already informed them. Then you can discuss with them directly everything necessary for future cooperation.

Antonio was delighted, "Everything is going like clockwork. You are our best organizer and our undisputed boss. No one can hold a candle to you. Are we finished now? I would like to see how Marian is doing and congratulate her to the wedding."

" Great, then let's go back upstairs."

Marian was pleased to see Antonio again. They had not seen each other for a long time. She knew Antonio since her earliest childhood and he had a special place in her heart. The two of them had taken a liking to each other since the very beginning. She had very much regretted that Antonio and his friendly entourage had been unable to attend her wedding. After she had greeted him warmly she asked, "And what about Karl, is he still working? He rarely shows his face lately. He just doesn't want to play tennis with me because he always loses and that annoys him a lot."

The father said to his daughter, "Marian, don't make your husband's life so hard. You know that he's not a good loser, but besides he's a great guy. If would be silly if the two of you argued because of a stupid game of tennis."

The daughter replied smiling, "That won't happen. He loves me too much for that. I'll give him a call now so that he has the courage to join us."

Together they went to the terrace to have lunch. The kitchen had prepared many delicacies at the boss' instructions. Whenever guests were visiting, the food was particularly good. Don Rosso knew what his guests' favorite dishes were; he was simply a man of the world and a perfect gentleman.

Karl sat down with the lively company and was glad that his father-in-law had introduced him as his right hand. Even though, it was unclear to him why he had not been present at the meeting. This displeased him a little. The group ate and drank together and there was a lot of laughter. Antonio always told funny stories from the past.

By the time the butler served coffee and cognac, the gentlemen and the lady were already all a bit tipsy. That's why after the meal they all went to have a nap.

The following afternoon Antonio, Don Rosso and Karl went for a walk together on a secluded beach to talk.

"Can you tell me what is behind the big meeting on July 23rd?" Antonio wanted to know.

Don Rosso provided no precise information, "In order to avoid speculation, I don't want to talk about it yet. Please wait until the date. But tell me, how are things going with you, are there any problems in the business? We can talk here, no one can hear us, the coast is lonely and abandoned. You can see a stranger from miles away."

Karl was now flattered that he was allowed to participate in this confidential conversation. The world was good for him again.

"The Vietnamese are giving us a bit of a hard time," Antonio said. "These guys are so disorganized. You just don't know what is going on there. What a bunch of cigarette smugglers. We already tried to contact one of the bosses in one way or another, but no chance. They are either not an established group or they change constantly. We gave up with the cigarette trade and are leaving that to the Russians and Vietnamese now. We can do without unnecessary sacrifices. They crush each other for one cigarette carton. We are focusing on the other traditional markets. Let them kill each other for their stupid cigarettes. We are busy with other things, things that we make real money with."

Serjo Rosso, "Has it already got that bad? Yes, times are changing. In Asia it's the Indians who are trying to make our lives difficult and in Europe it's the Vietnamese gangs. It's a good thing that we formed a community of interests with the Russians and the Chinese. They accept us. Still! Just recently I reforged the alliance in Hong Kong. But I will talk to Michele, he has the best contacts to the German Bureau of Investigation, he should use that. So that the bureau lights a fire under the Vietnamese. After all, the lobbying is costing us a fortune."

Karl listened very carefully as the bosses talked about markets. It sounded as if the captains of industry were developing their strategies.

"Boss," Antonio said to Don Rosso, "tomorrow the meeting with the 2nd rank of the Italian group and my first official visit is taking place in Palermo. Will you be there?"

Don Rosso declined, "No, leave it, it is not the custom that I have contact with the second rank. You can do it very well by yourself. You have been announced as being the new boss so that'll do. It wouldn't be good if they got to know me personally and know my identity. Especially since this is right in front of my door. No, we'll leave that."

"Yes. I understand," Antonio said. "Then I will pack my bags tomorrow, go to the meeting and then fly back home again."

After they had walked along the coast for a few hours they drove back together to the Rosso villa again.

During the journey Don Rosso asked, "Antonio, are you still carrying your iron around with you in your pocket? Your jacket is completely baggy."

When Antonio opened his jacket and folded one side open, Karl saw a real gun on a boss for the first time. Antonio answered the question with an affirmative nod and said that despite having bodyguards, he considered this necessary and therefore felt safer. Don

Rosso laughed out loudly, "You perfectionist are sure to have a gun license, aren't you?"

Antonio drew his weapons ownership card out of his jacket pocket, "Here, because everything has to be completely legal."

Now the loud laughter of the three in the vehicle could hardly be overheard. Don Rosso was so amused that he could barely hold himself on his car seat. The three of them spent the evening together with Marian on the terrace.

The next morning, Antonio said good bye to everybody and the Rosso villa returned to its daily routine again. The next few weeks passed in this style until the 18th of July.

The couple and Don Rosso were sitting together at the breakfast table when the boss announced, "At last. The day after tomorrow is the big arrival day of the family members. I have had to wait a long time for this. Now we will see whether my son-in-law has organized everything properly and if everything works. His first major test! Tomorrow we will pack our bags and on Sunday we will fly to Dusseldorf!"

Karl was not surprised by the announcement because he had known about the big date for weeks now. He didn't seem to have any great concerns and was sure that everything would run well. He had planned everything too accurately, not even the slightest thing could go wrong. Marian was looking forward to seeing one or the other of her school friends. Thus they

were all already longing for the big day of the meeting to arrive.

Uncertainty arose in the boss about a possible bloody battle

Around noon on Sunday, the Rossos flew together to Dusseldorf. There they each had a suite in the best hotel in the city.

Old memories from the first meeting with his wife in an excellent hotel in Cologne were reawakened in Karl again. He would also have liked to have known which of his colleagues had taken over his former position at the bank. But it was no longer befitting his social status to turn up there again.

Otherwise, the day went by quietly and Don Rosso made no attempt to contact the family members. He didn't want to expose himself to any unnecessary questions before the meeting started on July 23rd.

They also didn't participate in the excursion programs planned by Karl, but rather made a trip to Hamburg. In the harbor city, they walked around the Alster lake in beautiful summer weather or strolled through the elegant shopping miles. Marian was already familiar with the city and was happy to stroll with her husband through the streets and the cafes in the city center.

Every so often the Don withdrew to give himself time to think about the upcoming meeting.

The three of them went on a tour of the harbor to relax. It was the first time that Karl had toured one of the world's largest harbors. He found it very impressive to see the world's largest cargo ship or huge cruise ships at close range. The tour gave them the opportunity to free themselves from thoughts about the exciting meeting.

However, the meeting was in the boss' mind constantly. He wondered what his family members would have to say and how they would accept his grand plan for the future of the family. He went through all possible responses from each member of the first rank, one after the other. The individual characters were too different. This was, after all, not a homogeneous group.

Don Rosso tried to imagine which of the parties would maybe agree without hesitation and which members would be doubtful thus potentially becoming easy prey for the ringleaders.

He didn't doubt his authority. However, his plan went beyond anything that had ever happened before in the Italian Mafia. Could this unique plan perhaps jeopardize his position after all? The whole thing threw up an endless number of questions.

First of all, everyone was to report on what was going on in the individual organizations of the world. Maybe there was still one or the other issue in the reports that would be good to use in his reasoning. The situation also needed a bit of luck.

He knew his members well and knew that the intelligent family members would lend him a sympathetic ear. But there were still also the fools, and they were the ones he was most afraid of. These people were unpredictable, Would they maybe even join together to become a strong team and work against him?

In any case, it would all result in a real test. Despite all the stability of the past, he, the top boss, could not fully rule out for sure that his decision would maybe not split the family into groups. Then the whole structure could be split up into different groups creating a considerable hazard potential.

Just imagine what would happen if the fools ran their own regime thus bringing all the other members in danger of being discovered by the legal system. Due to their limited point of view, they would maybe fall back into becoming a trigger-happy society engaging in one bloody battle after the other with the remaining members.

In addition, there was the possibility that other groups would now see their great hour coming and want to show their strength and power. Could the Chinese or Russian organizations maybe even now already be observing the Italians' weaknesses and no longer feel handcuffed by the agreements? Was the general agreement between the parties that had been maintained and built up over generations in danger?

The Italian Mafia was no longer the world's strongest association. In a final showdown with other organizations, they would probably be defeated. The old respect of Rosso's organization was to a large extent the reason why they still had a strong alliance with the

Chinese and the Russians. This connection represented a deterrent for new invaders from India or other countries.

But how would they react if the alliance would be terminated? Would a whole new division of the markets then have to be expected? An international bloody battle could arise in countless war zones. The number of victims could be vast.

How would this all develop? With these thoughts in mind, Don Rosso became a little hesitant. Should he rather give up his plan at the last minute? It wasn't too late to tell the members that the planned meeting was going to be just a cozy conference with a general exchange of ideas. But he rejected this idea he straight away. This was a good plan for the future and there were no significant reasons to give it up just like that. And after all, he wasn't just going to bow to a couple of fools.

He would now carry out his plan, no matter what it cost. Of this he was absolutely certain.

Karl spoke to Don Rosso who was lost in thought, "When will I learn more about your changeover plan? What exactly is it? I am excited and curious."

Don Rosso replied angrily, "Not here and now! Wait until the meeting! Moreover, this is nothing for the public. What a question. I never want to hear such a question outside of our rooms from you again! Have you understood me at long last?"

Don Rosso was now very angry. How could his so smart Karl ask such a sensitive question in public? Did he not understand the principles of the family? If this would happen again, it would result in consequences for his son-in-law. You could play right into the hands of district attorneys with carelessness like that. This is something that the boss could not let happen.

Don Rosso's nerves had already almost reached the breaking point anyway. Marian treated her father only with extreme caution because she realized how tense he was. She had noticed that this would not just be a simple meeting, but that they were probably dealing with bigger things. But in no way did she wanted to dig deeper.

After his father-in-law's harsh and clear statement, Karl didn't dare to address one single word to him all day long. The silence in the round was only interrupted by one short announcement from Don Rosso, "We are driving back to Dusseldorf to the hotel and then I want to be left in peace until Wednesday."

No one dared to say a word against it.

When they arrived in Dusseldorf at the hotel Don Rosso disappeared immediately and was not seen again during the next few days.

Karl wanted to visit his hometown and asked Marian to come with him to Cologne. The next day, they strolled along the Rhine in the old town enjoying the Rhine promenades in the sun. They had chosen a restaurant that had linden trees outside whose flowers exuded a slightly sweet scent.

"It's very nice here," Marian said, "These ancient harbor houses with their half-timbered buildings are beautiful. But tell me, what's all this about this famous Kölsch beer?"

Karl told her, "There are about 100 different traditional beers in Cologne that are only allowed to be brewed within the city limits. The brewing tradition dates back to the year 873. Kölsch is drunk by connoisseurs only out of 0.2 liter beer glasses. It is extremely important that when serving it, a head is created. Only this guarantees that the beer is fresh and the glass is clean. During the city's famous carnival days, Kölsch is already served in the morning." "But it also tastes wonderfully refreshing in the warm sunshine," Marian thought.

Countless tourists strolled along the Rhine promenades past them. The city is especially popular for the myriad of historic buildings from the Roman period and not least because of the World Heritage Cologne Cathedral. It didn't take long until Marian was so drunk that they had themselves driven back to the hotel in Dusseldorf.

Karl slept fitfully this last night before the big meeting. Strange dreams accompanied his sleep. His father-in-law also had a restless and short night.

The next day, all three met at the breakfast table.

"The show will start in a few hours. Are you well prepared, Karl?" asked Don Rosso full of inner tension. Karl replied reassuringly, "Sure, everything will be fine."

He brooded about what his father-in-law meant by that; after all, he wouldn't be holding a speech. So why should he be prepared for the big meeting?

The big debate of the international bosses started

July 23rd had finally come, the meeting of the family members of the first rank could begin. The dedicated members had arrived from all over the world and had been accommodated in different hotels located in different cities. Even the family members were now tense. They wondered what were the important things the big boss had to report about that made him call a general meeting.

Since arriving, they had not received one single message, something which also surprised them. It couldn't be something minor that was to be discussed here because the big boss would never call a meeting for that.

They had tried to swap ideas beforehand, but that didn't bring any results either. As Don Rosso had not given anyone any clue why the meeting was taking place beforehand, he managed to avoid all speculation.

Therefore, the family members had no choice but to enjoy the days leading up to the meeting together with their wives and children by participating in the activity programs booked by Karl.

On the first meeting day, a gold-colored sign with the inscription "Shareholders' Meeting of La Finette AG, Medical Technic" was mounted at the entrance of the hotel in which the Rossos were also staying. The sign gave the whole thing a respectable touch, as is customary for an honorable shareholders' meeting.

The security guards secured the areas against unauthorized access. The floor of the conference rooms and the entrances were monitored by Don Rosso's bodyguards. Uninvited people had no chance of getting anywhere near the place of assembly. The dignified bosses were picked up from their hotels by chauffeurs with large armored limousines and driven to the conference hotel.

A recreation room had been rented in the hotel especially for the bosses' bodyguards . They were also not allowed to enter the conference floor. Before dawn even, a security company had been busy installing the mobile shielding devices in the conference room. An electronic security checkpoint, as is known from airports, had been set up. It was forbidden to all participants to bring mobile phones, recording devices or weapons to the meeting room.

The chauffeur of the limousines drove into the parking garage of the conference hotel and, unmolested by outsiders, the bosses were taken to the conference floor via the director's elevator.

Bar tables and a wide range of beverages as well as a small buffet had been organized for the guests. They should be lacking nothing. Immediately after they arrived on the floor, they were led through the security checkpoint and asked to dispose of all unwanted things.

The hallway gradually filled with members and lively discussions developed amongst the guests. The old friends were, however, deliberately only discussing general events happening in the world. There were no words about business or even speculations about the reason for this event. Everything went like clockwork and according to plan. Karl's previous detailed organization now paid off.

Don Rosso was still sitting together with his daughter and Karl at the hotel breakfast table. A few times he was informed briefly by his personal bodyguards about the situation on the conference floor.

"Well done, my dear son-in-law," he said to Karl, "Everything seems to work well. You will have passed your first test with flying colors." Then the boss disappeared behind his newspaper again in order to hide his lines of worry behind it.

Marian said to her husband, "I have to go now. Today we women are visiting the zoo. I am very curious to see what that will be like. Hopefully the weather will keep, it looks a bit cloudy." "It'll be find and if it rains, there is still the enclosed area with its wonderful aquarium," Karl chatted casually. "Men! As if young women are interested in an aquarium," Marian said. "Okay, you are all very boring this morning anyway. I hope you have fun doing your business and your all-important men's meeting. Bye, see you tonight." "Take care, see you tonight," Karl ended the conversation and Don Rosso piped up from behind his newspaper, "Have fun and I'll see you later."

What a great farewell for Marian. She knew when men had business in their heads, women were completely superfluous. If a women would do that even once time, she would immediately have to pay for it. Marian disappeared, a little grumpy about the impersonal farewell.

After his daughter had left, one of the personal bodyguards approached Don Rosso and whispered softly in his ear that all the shareholders were now present. Thereupon, Don Rosso put his newspaper to the side and said, "Karl, you are going to go to the conference room and ask the guests to take a seat. I will follow in 15 minutes." Without a word Karl nodded and walked towards the director's elevator. There he was welcomed by a security guard and taken to the conference floor by elevator.

"Gentlemen, my name is Karl Rosso and my father-in-law has asked you all to take a seat in the conference room. He will join us in a few minutes."

A lively murmur rang out amongst the guests. So this was the son-in-law! At the same time, they moved towards the conference room to take their seats, however, not without first taking a closer look at the new family member.

After the men had sat down and placed their nameplates on the tables in front of them, Don Rosso appeared in the room. Behind him the door of the mobile bug-proof cage closed. Then the guards closed the room doors from the outside. A crackling tension could be felt in the room. When Don Rosso entered the room, the attendees' murmuring became silent.

"Good morning, my dear friends," the great Don Rosso started. He radiated undisputed authority. "It's good to finally see you again after such a long time. I am very pleased. From what I can see, you are all alive and kicking!" The big boss had thought up a few personal words for each of them.

As he was sitting at the beginning of the row, Don Rosso first walked to Giuseppe who was responsible for the transfer of funds. He began the traditional ceremony with the Don stretching out his right hand and Giuseppe shaking it heartily before bowing over to kiss it.

"My dear friend Giuseppe, I still can remember how you used to foul me at football in school. But forgive and forget, my dear man. It is already more than two years ago since we met last."

Then Don Rosso moved along the row to Davide who was responsible for the US and began with the same greeting, "Davide, are you still in this world with your Texas hat? How are your dear wife and kids? I haven't seen you all in such a long time. I am pleased that everything is going well for you."

The next was Filippo who was in charge of the world's drug trade, "Well, my Beautiful Filippo, I see, you haven't changed. You are doing a good job. I suppose you have everything under control? I am also glad to see you again at long last." The Beautiful Filippo was all smiles and showed his admiration for the

Don with a Sicilian kiss on the hand.

Don Rosso proceeded on one step to Nicole, "My old friend Nicole, you have been in Asia for so long and still don't have slitted eyes, how is your gout doing?" "Big Don Rosso," Nicole replied, "The Asians do indeed have a wide range of medicine, but I have not found the right one yet. Cobra juice helps a bit. But why should I complain, that doesn't help. No, you learn to live with it."

"My dear Nicole, I think you have been hit by one of the toughest draws here. Everything has gone wild for you. Everyone is trying to push you out in Asia and you seem to have dead bodies every day. I thank you for your good work and your support of our family members."
Then Don Rosso moved on to the next one saying, "My distinguished Diego, I know Africa is a difficult place too. How is your pretty black wife doing? I hope to see her in the next few days. You surely heard about Eduardo's fate in Johannesburg, haven't you?" Diego nodded and after shaking hands he also showed his respects by the hand kiss as all the others had done before him.

The big boss now walked around the top of the conference table to get to the opposite side. There he approached Antonio who was now not only in charge of Europe, but also Italy. "Antonio, did everything go well at the meeting with the Italians? How nice that you came to visit us recently . Did you get home again without any problem?" "Everything is going real swell," The European boss replied.

The personal greeting ceremony took more time than Karl had included in his schedule. He followed the boss without saying a word. As a greeting, he also shook hands briefly with everyone. A little impatiently he stood behind his father-in-law, biting back pushy words.

The next man whom his father-in-law greeted was Michele. He was responsible for the lobbying business. "Did you bribe all the politicians again? You live an enviable life. You are present at every banquet and have discussions with all the big shots of this world. Good work, my dear, we are in your debt."

The boss quickly scurried past Eduardo's empty place where they had place a flower bowl with a funeral ribbon. He went to the next chair where Marco sat, the boss of the protection racketeers. "As I heard, apart from a few confrontations with rivals, your world is all in order. Are you still playing the piano as much?"

After Marco's show of respect, the boss marched on. "And last but not least my dear Luca. Now I come to you, my gambling friend. If we didn't have you and your casinos ... you build splendid palaces. You are doing great work for us. You and your fellow player Giuseppe really do a good job. You both are saving us the big worry that we have with money laundering. If we didn't have you two ..."

The last member also showed his respects to the boss and with that, the greeting procedure was completed.

Karl and Don Rosso went to their seats at the head of the conference table. The boss sat directly next to Diego and Karl was on his right. Don Rosso paused briefly and again the guests started to discuss amongst themselves. Everyone had something to report or asked about the well-being of the other. As a precaution, Karl had had the originally planned microphones on the participants' tables removed. "You have done well," his father-in-law praised. "It was farsighted to have thought about removing the microphones so that we don't receive the recording of a conversation as a gift from the hotel afterwards." After a while, Don Rosso stood up. There was immediate silence in the room.

Then he started his speech, "My dear family members, thank you very much for responding to my call to this meeting. We are, of course, all happy to see each other again after such a long time. I will keep it short. You all received the agenda. Before I introduce my son-in-law and assistant to you, I would like to observe a short minute of silence for our longtime friend and companion Eduardo. As you all already know, he sadly passed away due to a viral infection during a special mission to Africa. Let us remember him in silence. His wife and offspring will, of course, want for nothing. I informed her that she will continue to receive her payments as usual. Please let us now observe a minute of silence."

No sooner had the minute of silence passed, Don Rosso continued, "As you all know, the costs for such an event are very high. I thank my son-in-law, Karl, quite warmly for his help. Karl married my daughter Marian a short while ago. I desperately needed his support because everything was slowly becoming a bit too much for me,. My son-in-law is an organizational talent and he has a shrewd head so I scrutinized him carefully. He deserves the confidence of us all. I have taken the vow of unwavering and lifelong loyalty to the family from him. He is a confidant in our circle now just like everyone else here. In a few years, he will take over as my successor and I have assigned him with all the necessary powers. Before we start with the reports, I suggest we take a short half hour break. But please remember that we will open the room and therefore no more confidential discussions should take place. Please abide by that."

Karl was totally surprised that his father-in-law had introduced him to the assembled team as his successor.

Until the doors had opened some people in the round discussed briefly Eduardo's unforeseen death and how quickly it was possible for one of their round to say farewell forever. Others, still surprised, discussed the fact that Don Rosso had introduced an outsider as a new member and his successor. In their opinion, this didn't correspond in any way with family tradition. Some felt it was even a violation of the law of the clan. They were already wondering if this was the real reason for the meeting.

But when Don Rosso personally opened the door of the mobile safety cage and after that the room door, the talkative people grew silent. No word should leak outside. They all flocked to the heavily guarded hallway of the conference floor in order to help themselves to the buffet.

"Karl, we are still within our time plan?" Don Rosso called out to him. "Slightly over, but I think we will be able to catch up," was the reply.

The family members, all disguised as shareholders of La Finette AG, Medical Technic sat at the tables in discussions about private affairs: wives, children, the good weather and everything that friends tell each other when they have not seen each other for a long time. Karl was amazed how automatically the veil of silence had been drawn over the guests as soon as the security door had opened. It was indeed a perfect spectacle that had been rehearsed for decades.

The reports caused a stir in the minds of some of the participants

When the short break ended, the team returned to the room and the doors closed again. Don Rosso began with the introduction, "The conference is a shareholders' meeting of the Paris company in which you all hold shares. Karl Rosso is one of the board members there so we can act officially as a shareholders' meeting. Let's begin with the statement of affairs of each individual member. I give the floor to Giuseppe. Please, my money specialist!"

"Thank you, Don," said Giuseppe and continued, "Dear Don Rosso, dear friends. What I can report about the situation regarding cash transfers is that it is becoming more and more difficult and costlier to gather the funds and launder them in other countries for our organization. In Europe especially, the money laundering laws have become so strict that it takes a huge effort to collect it and bring it to companies or banks beyond international boundaries so that it is fed into the legal channel. Even our fellow bankers are more and more afraid to accept the funds. We constantly have to come up with new ideas and are incurring high loss ratios. The customs officials are keeping tabs on us in every imaginable way. When cash is being deposited into bank accounts, even the smallest amounts of money cause us problems or have become completely impossible because every payment of more than 10,000 Euros is immediately reported to the tax authorities. If we weren't so fortunate to have the casinos, we would be choked to death with cash. Unfortunately, I cannot say how long this will continue to function."

Don Rosso was satisfied how everything was playing into his hands. The problem of money laundering was something he could use well for his argument. Then he took over the discussion again, "That's not good news, Giuseppe. We will have to figure something out. What does it help if we earn money that we can't integrate into a legal channel. Does anybody else have an idea or any questions?"

They all looked at each other helplessly. After a short time the silence was interrupted by Filippo who said to everyone, "This is all kid's stuff! Don't act stupid, Giuseppe. We have always had these problems. Michele will have to help out a few of those high-ranking customs officials with money. That's his job."

Michele shouted back, "Yeah, you little idiot. You can easily open your mouth. You have no clue about how hard it is to bribe these guys. Do you think that they simply take the cash and disappear? This a job that takes years. They all, and especially the younger gen-eration, takes their jobs very seriously."
"Quiet!" Don Rosso interjected, "It will not get us any-where if we start pointing fingers at each other. Calm down. Let's listen what Davide from the US has to say. Please, Davide!" "It's not any easier there either," the American boss said. "The FBI is chasing us and the NSA listens in on almost every call. But what should we do? We need to react quickly and don't have the time to work with encrypted messages. The bosses of the third rank and their people are being exposed by

the dozen. The only thing that saves us is the respect that we have taught the guys mercilessly. I couldn't say though how long this will continue to work."

Again Filippo, one of the simple guys from the circle, called out into the room, "Another one who doesn't understand his job. Send me one of your people so that we can set an example. Believe me, we can do it. When he returns from Mexico into your sacred world with a boa constrictor around his neck, no one will doubt our authority anymore." "Damn it!," Don Rosso yelled at Filippo. "Do you think we are all stupid here? Your methods may be suitable in the drug business, but we work using our heads. It's not just there for drinking. Thank you, Davide, for being so open with your information." Then he asked Nicole, the Asian boss to the floor asking Filippo first to calm down. The drug lord though didn't find that funny and he documented this angrily by wheezing loudly.

Karl was completely surprised about how things in the round were developing. He had not expected that the family members would almost tear each other apart. As civilized as everything was on Don Rosso's premises, here in the round he experienced brutal arguments between the members. Despite the previous shows of respect towards Don Rosso, he was having problems putting oil on troubled waters. The whole situation was like an overheated kettle of emotions. It was possible that hidden personal feuds of an unknown background were being fought out.

Nicole took the floor, "From what the previous speaker was saying, you live a quiet life. For us, things are boiling over every hour. Our police are maybe not as technically well equipped as yours, but what we have are wild territory conflicts. The Indians and Koreans are forcing their way into our home territory. The Vietnamese and Cambodians also want to have a piece of the cake. Every day we have to defend our territories with weapons and wild shootouts. If we didn't have the agreement with the Chinese and Russians, we would have been pushed out of the game long ago. At this point I would like to thank Don Rosso again for recently renewing the agreement in Hong Kong through personal engagement." "Thank you for your kind words," Don Rosso said and gave the floor to Diego, the African boss.

"Nothing new from Africa," he said. "only that we can achieve little revenue, because people really have no money there. However, the new pirate gangs in Somalia are very successful and are chucking their money about. I thought about going into this business, but we will be unable to gain a foothold there. They are so highly equipped that we would need to fight against an army. Better to stay out of it." Filippo couldn't keep still. He jumped up and gave the floor to himself again, "For once in a lifetime they have the chance of good business on their doorstep in this damned, poor Africa and then they don't use it. This is too much for me, I don't understand it. Maybe I should take over that job!"

Don Rosso intervened before Diego was able to reply, "Filippo, you have no ideas about the situation in Africa. Even the soldiers from the west who are responsible for the protection of commercial shipping

184

have problems with the pirates. So please, Filippo, finally keep your big mouth shut when it comes to things you know nothing about." "Do you really think that heroin dealers are pleasant and friendly people?" Filippo raged. "Lunch break," Don Rosso interrupted energetically. "We will all go to the hotel restaurant that remains closed today to other guests. Nevertheless remember folks, no business discussions outside the conference room."

Karl was pulled aside by his father-in-law, who whispered a few words to him, "You see, the lambs here are becoming sharks. Everyone wants the other's job. You have to keep a tight hold on the reins in the arena. But it will really get hot when we start the open discussion round. I am excited to see what they are going to hit me with when it comes to you. But now let's first go and eat."

The overheated tempers were supposed to calm down during the lunch break

At lunch, the champagne flowed freely and the finest crustaceans were served. The participants has already forgotten the arguments that had taken place in the room. Even Karl enjoyed his food and had already found a good friend in Antonio.

Only Don Rosso was deeply lost in his thoughts and let the morning run through his mind again. He sat at the table together with Marco and Luca who were talking about the latest football results. Luca was a noted comedian who was also able to tell the latest jokes. Marco and Luca amused themselves at the top

185

of their voices and their constant laughter tore Don Rosso out of his thoughts. He didn't feel like laughing.

He thought about his battle plan for the next day. Things were actually going quite well, everybody reported about problems and fears for the future. This exactly fitted into his strategy. The participants' fears for the future also helped to support his idea.

During the next conference day, he would summarize the reports exactly in the way he needed them. He could integrate the problems well as a basis for the presentation of his future plans for the year 2020. Thus, he was getting closer to his goal. He had often wondered during the past few days and weeks how the meeting would go, but had not expected that fate could play right into his hands. His dark mood vanished.

Karl had already had his espresso after his delicious meal when he got up from the table and asked to be excused. He quickly went out to the front of the restaurant and, as expected, pulled his mobile phone out of his pocket. "Marian," Karl murmured, "I'm glad I reached you, we are just having a lunch. I didn't even have time to call you quickly earlier on." She replied, "I thought you had already forgotten about me and that I would have to take one of these gorillas as company for dinner." "I'm sorry," her husband whispered into the phone. "there is so much to do here, but you know that I am always thinking about you. You were so lucky with the weather. It's perfect for a visit to the zoo." His wife replied, "Yes, we are having a lot of fun here, it's really a nice place. The children are having fun with the small animals in the children's zoo and the sea lions are so cute. I would like to come here again with you sometime."

Marian's comment made him happy and he replied, "Then I chose the right program for you! I'm glad that you like it, but I have to go back now, we'll be continuing soon. I'm sending you a big smooch and I'll see you this evening, my dream woman."

Don Rosso waved at a bellboy to come closer. In good hotels, these people are responsible for calling visitors inconspicuously using a sign. The boss asked him to summon the guests back to the conference room in a competent manner. Don Rosso gave him a handsome 50 Euro tip. Thereupon the boy crept through the ranks and told everyone that they were expected back in the conference room shortly.

The guests followed the request at a leisurely pace and made their way back to the conference room. When the doors had shut again, Don Rosso gave the floor to Antonio. "After Eduardo's sudden death I, as European boss, have also taken over his activities in Italy. I think it fits quite well that way. In the past few weeks I had already spoken with the Don personally about the Vietnamese who are completely messing up our cigarette smuggling activities. We have now stopped being active in this business division so that we are not in constant conflict with this gang over trivialities. Everything else is going well and we are showing growth. We have no problems with any of the other big clans, everyone is deliberately keeping to the agreements and staying in their home territories. However, the technological equipment of the police force is developing so quickly that they will probably be as state-of-the-art as ours in the next few years. Therefore we can't afford any major escapades. Thank you for your attention."

It was clearly to be heard that Antonio had a higher level of education. Refreshed from lunch, Filippo leapt up again from his seat incensed, "Can someone tell me where we are doing business at all? You let yourself be pushed out of our very own cigarette business because of a gang of Vietnamese? I'm probably going to be the only one in future who is operating his business successfully and I will have to feed the whole family myself. Imagine if my competitors find out about the weaklings I am allied with."

Don Rosso interjected, "Filippo, please! We no longer live during the days when we solved all our problems with a gun. We work with our heads. This is also very important. Why do you think we are still respected by the Chinese and Russian clan bosses. We would be long inferior to them in terms of masses of people and brutality. In the end, we need to think about our wives and children. And anyway, nobody in this room is a spring chicken any more. So please, it's not as if we're starving."

This interjection was the first preparation for the summary for the next day. Don Rosso had already now laid the foundation stone for his future discussions.

"The Don is absolutely right," Michele cried out with Marco's consent from the back.

188

"If we continue like this, we will soon need to plan three weeks for such a meeting. We want to be able to come to an end today too," Diego also added probably thinking about his black wife who was waiting for him. "Silence," Don Rosso's voice echoed through the conference room, "yes, this is not going to work. If this continues, we will do it like in school, by lifting a finger. So Michele, you have the floor. Please."

Like a professional speaker, Michele waited until everyone in the room had calmed down again. He took part in training courses in rhetoric so he knew exactly how to gain the necessary attention from an audience. Then he began his speech, "Don Rosso is exactly right. My work would be much more difficult if we started behaving like gunfighters again. After all, the police is tolerating us quite well in some areas according to the motto: better them than uncontrollable others. This is the only way that we can do our business in peace. Like I said, bribery alone doesn't work these days. We can only get individuals who have fallen under difficult times under our wings with painstaking work. Do you remember the former German chief of the Federal Republic of Germany? It didn't take long and he was exposed by the press. The preparatory work dragged on for years. So we need to do everything very carefully. You can open up too many cans of worms too quickly that can never be closed again. Thank you!"

Karl was impressed by Michele's speech. He decided he would refresh his own rhetoric skills again sometime in the future by visiting a training course. "Okay, so that we make some progress here, may I hold the floor?" Marco asked. "Alright, Marco, I give you permission to talk," Don Rosso said in order to ensure that there was no loss of authority through the unauthorized freedom of speech.

Marco positioned himself and began, "Guys, I feel as if I'm at a medical conference or at a proper share-holders' meeting, where industry captains spout pretty words. I mean we must bear in mind that we are the Italian Mafia. We have old traditions. I am thinking of our ancestors; they would turn over in their graves if they could hear us here. But still, we are moving in safe water with our protection racket. It's only in Europe that we unable to gain a foothold. The people are just too stubborn, they would rather lose their lives than pay. No idea what goes through their minds. Perhaps we will come up with an idea for the future. That was it, my friends."

"Very interesting, dear Marco, Thanks for your explanation and now the next one, Luca." Don Rosso pointed at him. "That's not fair!" Filippo rumbled again in the round. "Are you going to exclude me from this round entirely? I have listened long enough to all this chatter. Now it's my turn!" "For the last time!" Don Rosso called out to the room in his pithy voice, "This is not the way it works, Filippo. We are not on the street here with second-rate criminals. Remember this once and for all – here I'm the one who gives you the floor. No one else. Is that clear, Filippo? Also for you? Or do I have to sanction you?"

There was now absolute silence in the room. The boss

had finally demonstrated his full authority. Karl had been surprised all day how the big boss had been able to hold himself back. But now he had clearly communicated to the participants that there was only one boss of all bosses in the room. The wily Don Rosso had just been waiting for an appropriate suitable situation to demonstrate his authority properly. Unexpectedly, there was applause for Don Rosso's words and the old rank order was reestablished.

"So, please, Luca!" Don Rosso said to the casino boss. He stood up and began, "We are, of course, also getting more and more competition in the normal business of the casinos. But that does not bother us because our principal focus is on money laundering. However, we are a bit cut off because Giuseppe cannot supply us quickly enough. In addition, it's more difficult to get replenishment from the players who in the end are the ones who flush the money into our channels. We are being closely watched, but we are very careful that nothing happens there. However, we could launder much more money. But I can understand the problem that Giuseppe described to us earlier on very well. In the US, they are also constantly chasing after illegal earnings. They have even forced Switzerland to lift their banking secrecy. But all in all we are satisfied. Thank you." "Thank you, Luca!" Don Rosso said. "This clearly confirms Giuseppe's words. And now finally it's your turn, Filippo."

Filippo had no need to be told twice, and started, "Dear Don Rosso, dear friends. The drug business is also changing lastingly." He was now trying to soothe the boss with his friendly manner and express himself with chosen words. "Chemical shit is being thrown onto the markets all over the place at low prices. Good cocaine has become simply too expensive. A chemical laboratory where this stuff is made is being set up in every corner of the backyard. Those damn pills are doing people in, but what can you do? We have to keep up with it or else we are out of business. You can only sell good cocaine to the high society. The FBI is chasing us, especially because these filthy pills are harming people so much. The world is certainly changing rapidly."

With that, Filippo ended his contribution but he couldn't resist complaining briefly about the fact that he had been the last person to give a report even though he was sitting at the front. When it became obvious that nobody in the round was interested, his annoyance quickly disappeared. "Let's take a short coffee break outside in the corridor," suggested Don Rosso. This was urgently needed because it wasn't just the cigar smoke in the meantime that was making the air too thick to cut.

Again, Karl was pulled aside by his father-in-law so that he could talk to him. "Karl, did you see? It's like a shark pool. You have to be careful they don't run riot. There are a lot of different characters gathered here. The differences make a consensus really hard." "I have been observing this all very closely," Karl said. "However, I didn't think it would be like this. It's very difficult to keep them at bay. I'm very excited about what you are going to present as your future plan tomorrow and how they will react." Don Rosso replied, "You can be sure, tomorrow things will really get going. It's going to be a difficult day for me."

After the doors and windows opened, everyone went out into the corridor of the conference floor to get coffee and cookies. All business discussions fell silent again as soon as the doors opened. After about fifteen minutes, the boss asked everyone to return to the room again.

When the room doors were closed again, Don Rosso stood at the head of the conference table and began, "Dear friends, today we have gone on a bit later than actually planned. But some of the information was probably very important for us so that we get an accurate idea of how our business is progressing. We can all see that it is not getting easier for any of us. Tomorrow I will talk about my new plan for the future. I think, so that tomorrow we get back to our families earlier, we should begin already at 10 o'clock in the new conference hotel."

Without a pause he continued, "According to the agenda that you all received I have scheduled separate meetings with each of you for Friday. Saturday is the family day when we are all going to take a boat trip together and then spend time with our wives during a dance and entertainment evening. I hope this meets with your approval. At this point I would like to thank my son-in-law, Karl, for his assistance in the organizing of the event. I think he has stood the test. With this in mind I wish you a nice evening. Tomorrow morning you will be picked up by the chauffeurs and driven to the conference hotel. I'll see you tomorrow." They all scrambled towards the exit door without another word.

"I am very tired," Don Rosso said to Karl, "I will probably only eat something quickly and then go to bed. It is going to be a tough day tomorrow."
"I can understand that well," the son-in-law replied. "Let's go straight to the new hotel. I had the luggage taken there already and I think Marian is already expecting us."

The boss nodded curtly and they took off for the new hotel. During the short drive, Don Rosso praised Karl that it had been a good idea to always have rooms at the meeting hotels so that they wouldn't have to drive around in the morning.

After the meal, the father-in-law immediately retired to his suite. Marian told Karl details about her funny day. However, she quickly realized that he was very tired from the long day and they also decided to go to bed early. For Karl the previous day had been very exciting and he processed the conference in his dreams rolling back and forth in his bed. He kept getting out the bed rousing Marian out of her sleep.

Next door, the sleep of the father was also frequently interrupted. The night's rest ended early for Don Rosso and he tried to refresh himself by swimming a few laps in the hotel swimming pool.

The next day, the three Rossos met at breakfast in the hotel restaurant. "Good morning," the Don's voice was to be heard. "Good morning daddy," Marian said. "I also wish you a good morning," Karl said. Marian began with to speak, "When I see how sleepy you two still are, it must have been a terrible meeting yesterday." Only a slight stammer came from the two gentlemen. "It was hard work yesterday, but let's have breakfast in peace."

Karl helped himself lavishly at the buffet, but Don Rosso only drank coffee and a glass of orange juice. With her usual patter Marian tried to persuade her father to eat, but without success.

After saying Marian a brief goodbye, the boss went with his son-in-law to the meeting area of the new hotel. As on the previous day, the other conference participants had been driven to the new hotel by the chauffeurs and were already in attendance. After a short check, Don Rosso announced completeness of the participants and the room doors were closed.

The top boss' presentation was explosive enough

"I wish you all good morning," Don Rosso started his great speech. He seemed to be tired and it was obvious that his night had been very short. Deep shadows under his eyelids were evidence of his fatigue.

Today was his big day, the day he had prepared himself for for so many months and that had caused him countless headaches. Would he be able to assert himself today? Could he convince his friends of his idea? Would they all agree to participate in this plan?

"Shall we begin?", was his next sentence. "Yesterday evening I thought about your stories again. If I draw a summary from them, I realize that we are all encountering problems."

For strategic reasons, Don Rosso began with Filippo's contribution in order to soothe the fool a bit and to get him on his side, " Filippo's report in particular gave me a lot of food for thought. As you all know, our grandfathers also never wanted anything to do with the dirty business of drug trafficking. But as soon as the ban on alcohol was lifted in the US, they decided on this as a quick replacement. This does not actually fit in with our traditions. After all, we originally gained the approval of the populace through creating our own kind of law and order in Sicily with honor and respectability. It can't be that we destroy the labor of young people very early because we are selling them this dirty stuff for easy money."

Michele's interjection interrupted the speaker, "I agree with you totally, dear Don Rosso. It really can't continue this way. We are destroying ourselves by doing that."

"Thank you, Michele," Don Rosso's voice echoed through the room, then he continued speaking, "But please, do not interrupt me. Later after my report we will have enough time to answer all questions and share our opinions." Then he continued unperturbed, "I also find the problematic situation that we are taking in tons of money from our business, but are hardly able to integrate it into the regular cash flow because of continuously stricter laws to be questionable. Last but not least, there is more and more threat of being exposed by the legal system because of the state-of-the-art technology that police and district attorneys have. But what also worries me a lot is the intrusion of brutal new gangs, in particular from India and Asia. How long the Chinese and Russians will grant us their solidarity and respect is also questionable. I would be interested in your opinion in this matter."

First Filippo, who now seemed to be somewhat reconciled because the boss had given his speech some significance, began to speak "There have always and at all times been difficulties. We will overcome them. We are adaptable and have intelligent people to guide us in our ranks. Therefore we will cope with the problems." In his mind, Filippo had of course included himself as one of the intelligent people.

Antonio stood up and threw into the round for discussion, "I see it a bit different than my previous speaker. We have never been so exposed to technical bugging measures as we are today. These computers are able to do almost anything. If they tighten the laws any more, we will be sitting on a pile of money that we can't do anything with and the new drugs are pushing the district attorneys into top form. No one gets away scot-free."

Then Marco piped up, "These are really fucking times. In earlier days we pulled a gun, shot a few people and that was it. Today they come with rocket launchers and blow up an entire city block. What is the world coming to?"

Diego stood up, "Yes, exactly. It's the same for us. Just a few years ago black guys had nothing to eat and today they have so much cash that they can buy the best weapon technology. They have rocket launchers as well already."

Don Rosso intervened again, "I think we should take a short coffee break before we come to the most important issue and the real reason for the meeting."
He wanted a few minutes of rest so that he could compose himself again. After all, the future of the clan depended on his next words. He could now use a few minutes of concentration. Everything was open. Would the team pounce on him and tear him apart when they heard his proposal or would they together all support and understand his plan? All options were open and the next few minutes would decide whether his plan was successful or not.

Again doubts arose again briefly in his mind. He could still go back. But then he realized again that his plan for the clan's future was the only and best solution. So he had to overcome all doubts and press on regardless. The minutes passed by and as soon as he was sure about what he was doing, the meeting couldn't continue quickly enough.

Unexpectedly, he urged the participants to hurry back now."Sorry, but we want to start again, so that we can maybe finish off a bit earlier today," Don Rosso said and began to move back towards the conference room. The others quickly finished their coffees and followed their boss hastily.

Doubts about the boss spread and an escalation threatened

Like a lone wolf Don Rosso stood at the head of the meeting table until silence spread out throughout the room and the doors were shut. He didn't even let himself be distracted when Karl addressed him briefly. He was tense and searched for the right words to begin his presentation. The participants also noticed that dynamite was in the air.

Only after the room was shrouded in dead silence that you could have heard a pin falling on the floor did Don Rosso begin, " I will summarize this briefly! Problems in the future will provide us with new challenges. Not even our dear ancestors had to deal with such difficulties at any point in time. That is why I arranged for this meeting so that we can take an important step into the future together. Your safety and that of your loved ones is something that is very dear to my heart. Especially since we have pursued all paths together and successfully during the course of our lives."

Now everyone was listening very carefully and anxiously. No one dared to make even the slightest sound. The decisive words should fall at last. Karl was tense and sweat broke out on his forehead. The tension in the room was unbearable. The boss of bosses started to present his plan to the audience, "Because my father put your future in my hands, I want to present you with a new and safe plan. A plan that will allow all of us to spend the rest of our lives in peace and harmony." He paused briefly to concentrate and wiped the sweat from his forehead. Everyone noticed that the words did not come easy for him.

Then he cleared his throat and continued with his speech, "Well, with far-sightedness we in the past invested our money well and made considerable investments in legal company participations. Today these significant investments offer us safe and legal income and allow us and our loved ones, our descendants and their descendants, to have a secure income. That means that, without other business dealings, we could continue to have this wealth permanently and without restrictions if ..." , now he took a deep breath to finish the sentence, "... yes, if we withdraw from all other business dealing."

Now it was out. He collapsed inwardly. At first, the room was still totally silent. No-one knew yet how to react to the boss' words. What the boss had said a minute ago had not yet been processed. There were a few minutes of calm until Luca spoke up first, "Did I understand that correctly? We should withdraw from all business dealings?" Hearing this, Filippo jumped up from his chair, "You can't be serious! What if companies all of a sudden don't pay any money anymore? Do we then apply for welfare? That can't be!" Don Rosso stood like a culprit in the middle and didn't say a single word. He was wise and wanted the critics to let off steam before intervening again.

Antonio stood up slowly and deliberately and asked the others who were discussing amongst themselves to be silent for his speech, "Dear Don, my highly respected friend, for many years you have led our group successfully and responsibly, just like your father did before you, but we don't understand your idea at all. We are the oldest closed group, the only association in the world, that has existed for many generations. We can't just give that up. So far, we always followed you without hesitation, you have always been our undisputed boss, but now?"

The next one who wanted to add his comment was Davide, "This is really a very bad joke. Even if we wanted to, we couldn't get out that easily. How do you imagine that happening?" Even the quiet Nicole with his Asian charm couldn't stay still on his chair, "Where is our honor? We have to save the heritage of our ancestors for our descendants." he allegations against Don Rosso became louder and his authority in the group had already suffered. Could he still fight the rearing pack? Even Karl had made himself small behind his father-in-law and didn't dare utter a word. So that was what his father-in-law had hidden from him and all the others all the time: a complete retreat from all illegal activities. That is why the boss wanted to tighten control over the company's investments and monitor the companies more closely. He understood now why Don Rosso had not given him and all the others any notice in advance what his plan for the future was based on. The danger that wild speculations would have arisen in the run-up was simply too big.

The wise Michele stood up and shouted into the loud round "Silence, calm down everyone, we really can't discuss it like this," He waited until all eyes were fixed on him and added, "I think Don Rosso is not completely wrong. I can't even imagine how this plan can be implemented, but at least it's worth thinking about. Why should we continue in this business with the fear of being revealed when we can afford a good life without danger?"

For the first time Don Rosso got approval. Inwardly, it had upset him a lot that no one respected his authority anymore. A democratic deposing of a top boss had never taken place before in the history of the Mafia and was also not intended. Only a death could pave the way for a successor. Did Don Rosso maybe even have to fear for his life? Giuseppe who had been reserved till now announced, "I think Michele is right, we could at least discuss it. But I have no idea how this is going to work. Anyway, the boss is right; if we don't get the money into legal channels, then it's completely meaningless for us."

Filippo could now not bear sitting silently on his chair any longer, "Damn you, you chickens, first he introduces an outsider as his successor and directly afterwards he wants to disband our group. What else can we expect? Will you accept all this without contesting it? It's against all the old traditions that we have inherited from our fathers!" "Right!", Luca chimed in. "The Don has led us excellently for decades, but he has to realize that we cannot and do not want to simply say goodbye to our heritage like this."

"Everyone, just think about it," Diego pointed out, "If, as Don says, there is no need, why stick your necks out and then maybe get shot by one of the next gangs? If we can live in peace with the livelihood that we have then I don't necessarily need this thrill to be happy." Filippo pointed out again, "And what do we do then? Sit on the park bench in the evening and drink our beer and then go home to warm slippers? Or sing a song together with our children and wife?"

After listening to everyone for a while, Don Rosso piped up in his pithy voice, "Okay! Everyone has had their fun, but now we have to get some order here again. Filippo, now to you. Again, we are not on the streets here, pull yourself together. I will not tolerate - and listen carefully - I will not tolerate any insults. This is the last time I am warning you!"

He had waited for exactly for the right time for his action. On the one hand, the flared tempers had started to die down, on the other hand, he was able to clearly show who was boss. In addition, the time had come to show no weaknesses to his audience. With the general discussion, time was running out. They still had to have a lunch break. But it wasn't yet time for that. He had reckoned with even louder protests. The fact that one or the other had more or less taken his side was very convenient. Now he wanted to give the guys a little more time to think about his suggestion.

Karl was glad that his father-in-law once again had the upper hand. A little longer and the Don wouldn't have been able to hold his power as boss much longer. "When you have calmed down a bit, we can continue," Don Rosso exclaimed and went on further, "The whole thing will of course take time. Everything has to be planned precisely. Each of you will have enough time to adapt to the new situation. I am thinking of a period of seven years, in 2020 everything should be completed. A life without fear and still in luxury. Let's stop for lunch now and everyone can think about it again in peace and quiet. But one thing is clear: No one is allowed to find out about this. This afternoon, I will give you more details and tomorrow I have planned a full day for individual meetings with each of you. I hope you can still enjoy your lunch in spite of everything."

Hardly had the room doors opened, than some hotheads stormed angrily out of the room. A further group walked out to lunch leisurely and deep in thought. Don Rosso stayed back briefly with Karl. He addressed Karl, "Now you know what the plan is. I'm not feeling too well, I would like to get some rest in my room. Have some of that lovely food brought to my room please, thank you and I'll see you later. Oh, before I forget, no word to Marian. But I think you know that by now. I don't need to stress myself any longer."

Karl replied, "I do, you can count on me, boss. You have done well, Serjo. Respect!" Actually Karl was dying to tell his wife everything, but he knew that this could cost him his life. Therefore he meticulously kept to his promise. For once he didn't call his beloved wife during the lunch break as he usually did. That is something that his wife would reproach him for in the evening as being a serious misconduct. But now Karl went in the direction of the restaurant to take his lunch. He had phoned an employee at the front desk to order a meal to be sent to his father-in-law's suite and then he took a seat at a table with Antonio. As always when eating, all discussions about the meeting were taboo for the members of the meeting.

Better to die than to retire

Don Rosso only returned again two hours later. He entered the dining room in high spirits and rested and asked his family members to follow him back to the conference room. After everyone had taken their seats again and the doors were closed, the great Don continued the meeting. Since the participants had filled their bellies with relish, the talks now proceeded in a rather more dignified manner.

"Just think," Don Rosso started, "you will doing your descendents a good turn. After all, you will hand them over a life without fear. They will enjoy a life of luxury without ever having to put up with the fears that we are suffering every day of our life. Just think of the dangers that are lurking everywhere, be it a life prison sentence, a gang that is making attempts on our life or a traitor from the own ranks who wants to track us down. After the changeover, we could all make a new start and concentrate only on legitimate business. There is enough to do."

Even on a full stomach Marco, the boss of the protection racket, now joined in the conversation, "But we aren't captains of industry, we have no idea about this. Filippo is quite right, I also don't want to spend my day reading the morning newspaper and then watching my wife while she is cooking. Don, you have to understand that. We are not born for that."

Don Rosso replied, "You can learn everything. We have sufficient time to pick this up in peace and quiet.

Then you will see that the management of companies can also be exciting and fun. The only thing that you will be giving up is the danger of dying an early unnatural death or being visited by your grandchildren in jail only once a month. I personally see this as a very big step forward."

Antonio agreed with the Don and began, "Well, you must see this clearly, the Don is right. I can already imagine how well I am going to sleep at night without worries and troubles. After all, we are not getting younger and we already have our storm and stress period behind us. Don, you have convinced me, you have my agreement."

One by one, Diego, Giuseppe, Michele and Luca stepped forward with the words, "Yes, you also have my agreement, Don."

Don Rosso had already won half of the battle. Satisfied he looked at Karl, who was also extremely relieved. Now what remained was to win over the others. Only Nicole, the Asia boss, Davide, the US boss, Marco, the boss of the protection racket and the difficult Filippo with his drug business remained. Don Rosso wondered how he could win them over for himself. Could he already be sure about the support of those who had just agreed or was it all still touch and go? He had to make another move, although this could be risky and backfire.

Don Rosso continued with his speech, "I thank you for your approval, but a final vote will be made by secret ballot. I have scheduled this for Saturday after the individual interviews. You can continue your exchanges while I carry out the individual meetings. For that, I authorize Michele as temporary director of this round."

The choice of Michele was obvious as he had good qualities to chair the meeting and was rhetorically one of the best in the room. He had also thought about Karl, but because he wanted a strong leader in the meeting, that would have been a bit too early.

It was tactically clever that the group had the opportunity to discuss amongst themselves without the boss being present, especially because the supporters of his plan had already formed a strong group. There was maybe still one or the other who had his doubts about whether they could win short-term. After all, the maxim also applied in this meeting that a few bellwethers can lead a whole herd. But that of course could also be true in the other direction.

On the way to the reorganization there would be many bodies

"But there is one thing", the boss said loudly to everyone in the round, "that we have to determine so that everything is clear. If we want to do this, it will require the agreement of everybody in this round. Everyone needs to support it 100%. And to forestall the question, I will not put up with the family splitting up. Spin-offs are completely out of the question. That would be accompanied by far too great a risk for all of us. So that it's clear: it's everybody or nobody."

Filippo tossed in the comment, "That's what I thought!"

Giuseppe followed with, "But that's very clear; if somebody who starts his own business makes mistakes, then we are all in danger and we have no protection anymore."

Don Rosso confirmed this, "Thank you, Giuseppe, that is right. Of course, nobody, not even our allies, is allowed to notice anything about our intentions until the changeover has been completed. The risk that others notice weaknesses in our organization and take the opportunity to annex our organization for themselves, would be just too big."

"Then we have to cut off all rearward lines of communication and wipe out all confidants once and for all," pointed out Nicole, the Asia boss,.

Karl began to listen closely. What did Nicole mean by cutting off and wiping out all confidants? Did they want to wipe out all the go-betweens and their front men at once? How many of these so-called confidants did they have anyway?

"But that is going to be no easy undertaking," Davide immediately interjected, "after all, we are not talking about five or six people. And anyway, if they hear anything about what is happening and all act against us at once, what happens then?"

"Those are details we will still have to clarify," Don Rosso replied. "Everything has, of course, to take place at approximately the same time and before they find something out, but first we have to agree that we carry out the plan and then we have seven years to organize everything in detail. We can do it, I am absolutely sure about that. Friends, I think this was an exciting day for us all. Let's close the meeting for today and continue as usual tomorrow in the new hotel. I wish you all a nice evening and think again in peace and quiet about my words. I think that below the line it's best for all of us all to implement this reorganization. With this in mind, I'll see you tomorrow."

He went straight to the exit and asked Karl to follow him, "My dear son-in-law, now I need a cognac. I'm sure you do too"

Karl replied, "You can say that again, I need one too."

"The battle is not quite over yet," Serjo said, "but we are getting closer to the goal . I think once they have thought it through calmly, they will realize that this is the best way for us all. The only one who still worries me is Filippo. The fool will never understand."

Karl spoke softly, "If only I had known this all earlier. Too bad that you didn't tell me before. I could definitely have helped you. It actually all comes at the right time. I also would prefer to only take care of the legitimate business of the company investments."

"You have already helped me a lot with your moral support, my dear son-in-law. I already took a big risk in choosing you to be my successor. You heard that from Filippo. No, it's okay, everything went well. Thank you. " As soon as the Don had said this, they took the elevator directly to the hotel bar.

As they arrived in the hotel bar "Old England", Karl called out to the barkeeper, "Two double cognacs, only the best, please." The bar was furnished in old English style. Wide brown leather armchairs that were well padded invited guests to relax. The two men let themselves sink into them. The barkeeper served them the cognacs elegantly. They gulped down their glasses. "The same again and bill Suite Petersburg," Don Rosso called out to the barkeeper.

Karl took his cell phone out of his jacket pocket and called his wife, "Hi honey, we finished work a bit earlier today. Yes, we will be in the new hotel in one hour. It was a tough day for us all. See you later. Kiss!" He waited in vain for his wife to bawl him out for not calling during the day.

212

The barkeeper served the next round swiftly. As soon as they had emptied their brandy snifters, they both immediately feel the effects of the alcohol after their strenuous day.

Don Rosso stood up a little unsteady on his feet and said, "Come on, let's go on to the next hotel. I am tired and would like to freshen up a bit."

As soon as they arrived in the hotel for that night, Don Rosso retired after a brief farewell. Karl hurried to his wife in their suite. After a brief welcome, Marian started bawling him out and complained vehemently about the fact that her husband had not called her during the lunch break. Tired and exhausted Karl endured the never-ending reproaches. This was the first small argument in their short marriage. After his wife had asked him about how her father was, he took a refreshing bath and went to bed sleeping through to the next morning.

Suddenly, a knife flashed. Enraged, Filippo raced around the conference table to Don Rosso. The attendees were terrified and sat stone-faced. Snorting Filippo cried, "This is insufferable, I'm going to kill you."

As quick as a flash, Don Rosso pulled a small gun out of his jacket pocket and shot his attacker in the middle of the forehead. The attacker fell covered in blood onto the floor without uttering a sound. Then Karl heard his father-in-law say, "Anyone who dares to step out of line ends like this." The pressure went out of some of the attendees and they ran to Filippo who was lying motionless on the ground. "There is nothing to be done anymore," they cried out. "Unbelievable, what an idiot", Antonio said as he ran over to Don Rosso who could not stand on his feet anymore and stumbled onto one of the chairs.

"It really should not end this way," the supremo said. After a period of helplessness Michele asked, "What can we do now, we are not prepared for this at all."

However, Don Rosso was prepared for this situation, "I have a specialist for this kind of thing, he will take care of it." He pulled out his cell phone and dialed Francesco's number.

"Karl! Karl!" Someone shook him violently and incessantly. Still dazed and completely drenched in sweat he woke up next to his beloved wife who looked at him worriedly. "Karl, what's wrong? Did you have a bad dream?" Marian asked. Karl stood up and went to the bathroom. He had not had such a bad nightmare for a long time.

He stayed for some time in the bathroom and took a shower. When he returned, he said quietly to Marian, "I'm glad you woke me up, I had a horrible nightmare, my nerves are still frayed."

Karl had of course not been able to cope with his new stressful situation yet. Therefore, he was under constant strain and his nerves were as tense as wire ropes. There had been no life-threatening excitement like this in his previous life as bank organizer. He wondered whether, despite his new luxurious life, he had maybe not made a bad exchange after all. Maybe

214

his important physical organs would be unable to stand up to the stress. He asked himself the question whether he would be able to learn how to live with this burden permanently.

Marian caressed her beloved husband's head compassionately until he fell back into a deep sleep. She was now worried about her husband and she asked herself how her father, who had to spend every night alone, might be feeling.

Half rested, the Rossos gathered at the breakfast table in the new hotel. Don Rosso's bloodshot eyes were a sign that he had also not had a good night's sleep. Worried, Marian talked to her men, "Please take it a bit easy. After all, I want to have something more of you. Father, don't forget that you are getting on in years and Karl is already plagued by nightmares at night." But her words only bounced off the men who were deep in thought.

"The last working day for this week, let's go, Karl," came out of Don Rosso's mouth. Not forgetting to give Marian her obligatory kiss, Karl followed hot on the heels of his father-in-law.

What was certainly surprising was that the attendees were cheerful and in high spirits as Don Rosso and Karl entered the room. All of the members had returned and the heated discussions of the previous day seemed to have been forgotten. Nevertheless, Don Rosso and Karl didn't fully trust the peace. What were the participants up to?

The deciding vote of the members surprised the attendees

"My friends," Don Rosso began, "first of all, I wish all of you a good morning and hope that, unlike me, you all had a good night's sleep. We will now begin with the individual interviews. I suggest that we proceed according to the seating plan and that you all come separately, one after the other, into the room next door that we have organized specially for this purpose. We will start with Giuseppe and then continue clockwise. I have scheduled about an hour for each of you. Please adhere with this procedure. In the meantime, you discuss amongst yourself under the direction of the acting chairperson, Michele. Do you all agree?"

General agreement echoed through the room. Then Don Rosso stood up and Karl wanted to follow him, but his father-in-law sent him back. It would have been too much for his friends in this tense situation if Karl had participated in the confidential individual interviews. So Karl remained in the conference room and his father-in-law went with Giuseppe to the next room. The doors closed and even with the best will in the world, nobody was able to hear a word that the two confidants in the sealed room said.

Gallantly and honored Michele took over the leadership of the round. When the discussions threatened to escalate amongst the participants, he intervened briefly with soothing words. Karl saw that his father-in-law had indeed chosen the right person from the round to lead the assembly. In the maze of opinions, it was hard for him to recognize the general atmosphere in the discussion round. Everybody talked at once and the discussion moved back and forth amongst the dialog partners quickly and in an incomprehensible manner.

After an hour Giuseppe returned from the room next door and was visibly satisfied with his conversation with Don Rosso. Now Davide stepped forward quickly for his discussion with the Don. Not all of them needed a full hour for their meeting and by around noon, Nicole was already next. As an outsider, Karl deliberately didn't participate in the opinion-forming discussions between the family members. By lunchtime he could still not identify any clear opinion about the proposed reorganization. The participants' arguments went back and forth too wildly.

After the traditionally important joint lunch, the discussions in the room continued. Everyone who came back from the conversation with Don Rosso was in a good mood and Karl was sorry that he could not be present during the discussions. He would surely have been able to learn a lot from Don Rosso and his special way of dealing with all of the different characters. In any case, it seemed as if the big boss had found the right words for each individual. An attack on his position as boss or his unlimited powers was no longer to be expected. He had taken over the helm for himself again and no one would raise even the slightest doubt about his authority now.

More and more often, Karl heard the positive arguments for the reorganization outweighing the negative. Even the great opponent Filippo seemed to be acquiring a taste for the situation and took the side of those who had already given their consent gushingly and in high spirits. Nothing unexpected happened, his father-in-law seemed to have won the battle. But Karl didn't want to lull himself into a false sense of security too early, because he still could feel a certain tension and uncertainty amongst the family members.

Luca was the last to came back with from his individual interview with the boss. Don Rosso had wisely put his arm on Lucas' shoulder to express unity. Karl's father-in-law was a wise man and had everything planned down to the last detail. He was an artist in the field of man management. In Karl's eyes, his negotiating skills were not to be surpassed. The general atmosphere in the room was now more of a friendly nature and the previous day's violent arguments seemed to have been forgotten.

Karl and Don Rosso did not realize that in a secret session the evening before, the wise Michele had once more explained all the aspects of the reorganization and the positive arguments in full detail to the participants. He was able to show that the reorganization could only bring positive results for everyone involved.

"Your words were very enlightening," Don Rosso took over leadership in the round again. "You have all provided me with extraordinary information. I must confess, I have been convinced that we should have arranged such meetings more frequently in the past. A mistake on my part, I apologize for that. Nevertheless, your words have encouraged me even more that time is making it necessary to head for new shores. Therefore against the agenda and because we were able to carry out the individual interviews so quickly and with that win a lot of time, I would now like to begin with the casting of votes. Or does somebody in the round have any objection to that? No, very good! Let's begin with the secret casting of votes. As always, everyone gets a piece of paper to mark with a cross. „Yes" for going forward with the reorganization or „No" for the final burial of the plan. Let us vote. Karl, please hand out the voting papers now and then collect them in the container."

Karl did as he was told and gave each person a voting paper after which he gathered them back again from the voters. The task was completed quickly. No voting official was required for this small round, everyone could see the voting papers. Silence descended in the room. Everyone was excited about the outcome of the vote. After all, there was no doubt about the fact that only one single negative vote would ruin the entire plan. Could this difficult balancing act end positively for Don Rosso? The opponents of this activity had after all still been in the majority the day before.

"Michele, please start counting the votes," Don Rosso ordered. Nervously Michele opened the voting box and pulled out the first folded voting paper. "An agreement, a 'yes'." Despite the tension, the words came out quite loudly. Now it was like in a betting shop with the attendees all shouting out at once. Even

Filippo, despite his conflicting opinion on the previous day, had become a supporter.

Michele took the next piece of paper from the ballot box, to announcement, "Agree." Some of the attendees in the round shouted out a long-drawn "yes" as an expression of enthusiasm. Karl and Don Rosso stood stone-faced with folded arms behind the curious onlookers. The father-in-law had gained his composure again and was master of the situation. Karl admired his bearing and wondered whether he would ever be able to achieve such authority.

After a short time Michele's voice echoed again, "A 'yes'!" The situation repeated itself several times until the agreements predominated. Each "yes" was now supported by enthusiastic shouts from the voters. Slowly, a slight grin appeared on the two Rosso faces. Michele's next announcement was "agree"!

All the votes up to the last one were positive. The next moments would decide everything. Will the welfare for the families' future stand in the foreground or should they continue in future with their dangerous business dealings bringing their descendents an insecure life? A few more seconds and the decision about the future of so many people would be made. Not only the family members, but also their wives and children would be affected by this decision. Also numerous victims on the edge of the Mafia would be affected by a positive future. Other gangs would close the gaps quickly, but it would take time until the criminal business dealings would be occupied again.

Suddenly everyone heard Michele's voice, "And the last vote is ...", he made it particularly exciting by holding back a bit,"... Agree!" Now Karl could no longer hold himself back and roared, "Great, great. I don't believe it." He felt joy, he couldn't hold himself back any longer and jumped about in the air cheering as if he was in a football stadium.

The participants all gathered around Don Rosso and congratulated him with a handshake. Michele congratulated first and patted the boss' shoulder. He was followed one by one by all the others and last but not least by Karl. Don Rosso let himself be celebrated extensively and he beamed with pleasure. Now all the tension of the last few months fell off his shoulders at once. He had suffered a lot during the previous months because of uncertainty about how the voting would go.

Then he raised both arms high above his head and cried out, "Friends! Dear followers, you are all fantastic. I thank you so much for your trust and your insight. With this, the journey to new shores for our families is determined unanimously. I think we deserve a dinner together. Let's go!"

Exuberant, they all disappeared into the hotel restaurant and enjoyed the delicious food. Don Rosso and Karl were not aware of the fact that not only Don's speech, but also Michele's efforts were responsible for the good results. In any case, the vote had fallen unanimously for a reorganization. Karl was also delighted, but regretted that he couldn't celebrate this success together with Marian. He didn't want to be bawled out by his wife again in the evening and therefore dialed her phone number before eating, "Hi sweetheart, we are just having a break. How are you?"

She replied, "Fine so far. After you left this morning, I went back to bed and had a good sleep. Now I am sitting here with Michele's wife in a cafe and we are chatting. But tell me, how is everything with you and how is father doing?"

Promptly the husband replied, "Your father is also well, everything is going really well. Your father is doing great. We are through with the topics so far. Tonight we will be celebrating our good results. Your father and I are overjoyed. I'm really hungry now so see you later, I love you, my beauty." Then he went into the dining room.

Don Rosso had all the tables placed in the middle of the restaurant for the celebration. All the family members sat together while eating. Now they were a large family again, the harsh words that had been exchanged during the last few days were forgotten by all. "Let us celebrate, friends, play our Sicilian music and revive old memories" Don Rosso called out exuberantly.

The men started dancing to the sound of the music. Exuberant and happy that the dispute had ended relatively mildly, they behaved like kids. Some of them had good voices and sang with the music. Only now could you really notice that these gentlemen had spent all their lives together and had so much in common. The first jokes from their youth started falling and they remembered the pranks that they experienced together. This was a tight-knit community, just like a family, even though most of them were not related.

They were simply an honorable family, a tight-knit community that was also able to overcome problems. But it would have been extremely unfortunate if this togetherness failed because of the question about the future and a possible war arose between the participants. The participants enjoyed the private party for more than two hours until one of them remembered the issues that were still outstanding and reminded them that they should continue their day's work.

Slowly and somewhat sulkily they trotted back to the conference room. They would have liked to have continued partying but had to admit that they should resume their work. "Dear family members," Don Rosso continued opening up the round again, "thank you wholeheartedly for the small but refreshing celebration in the restaurant earlier on. I have been thinking about our time and the long path we have taken together. I must confess, my Sicilian heart has also been reinforced. I feel great joy about the fact that I can lead you and your children and grandchildren into a new secure future without fear. The matter is of course not resolved only with the decision. There are still many detailed questions but I am sure that with the great support of my son-in-law, we will achieve this together."

Don Rosso paused briefly to take a sip of water from his glass on the lectern. Then he continued, "It will of course not be an easy task, especially because, as of a certain date, we have to break off all the old connections from the past. In addition, you are going to need to learn a lots of new tasks. But we have plenty of time to do so. I think seven years will be enough. Indeed, we all are not getting any younger and for one or the other of us, it will be slowly be time to go into retirement. To conclude this, I would like to say one more thing. I have learned a lot from our meeting and your words and that is why in future, I would like to hold a regular annual meeting. These will also give me the opportunity to explain to you the next stages of our journey into the future. Please understand that after a very busy week, I must get a little rest this evening and that we will meet again tomorrow on the boat tour."

Now the whole team stood up and applauded their boss heartily. Karl had not expected the meeting to be like this. He had been of the opinion that the boss would dole out instructions that the members of the first rank would carry out without asking any questions. But as he discovered, the Don led his subordinates in a democratic way, or at least seemed to. It was hard to imagine what would happen if his authority would be put to a hard test. Karl's father-in-law was an odd person who never really opened himself up to anyone. He even kept a certain level of reserve towards his daughter. He was probably not in a position to make his feelings obvious.

Karl was looking forward to at long last being able to spend a leisurely evening with his beloved wife again. This suited them well. When he entered their hotel room, Marian lay in provocative clothes on the bed in order to beguile him. She had had to do without him

224

for so long. She only allowed him to take a quick, refreshing shower before she literally devoured him.

Later that evening, Marian called her father on the room phone and asked if he would eat with them in the hotel restaurant. He accepted the offer gratefully and they met a short time later. Don Rosso was in a great mood. Karl had not seen him so unrestrained and happy in a long time. In order to celebrate the day, they emptied one bottle of red wine after the other. The father began to sing songs and Marian joined him. Karl had never seen either his wife or his father so exuberant before. When the waiter came to the table and asked them not to disturb the other guests in the restaurant, the three of them returned to their suites.

Saturday started off with sunshine. When the family arrived at the boat for the river tour, the members of the first rank were already there with their wives and their children. The many children romped around together on the boat. When it took off the atmosphere was fantastic. The white-painted excursion steamboat shone in the sun and a band began to play on the open deck. The wives had put on their most elegant dresses and their men stood together in dark suits. The ladies drank champagne and the gentlemen whiskey. The steamboat went up the river towards the Siebengebirge Mountains making a wonderful day trip for the guests.

As the grand finale of the day, a big party in the ballroom took place in the evening. Now old ties were welded together again. All the disputes or discrepancies of the last few days were forgiven and forgotten.

In the ballroom, Don Rosso drew Karl to the side and said, "My dear Karl, you are a great organizer. It has been a really successful day and amusing for everyone. Thank you very much for your support. I owe you a lot. As I said some time ago, you and I are an absolute dream team. I am curious whether we will also be able to handle the rest of the difficult mission just as well together."

The last party guests of the party only went home at dawn. It took them almost the whole Sunday to recover again.

The final meeting led to new surprises

None of the Rossos was prepared for a surprise at the final meeting on the Monday morning. Don Rosso entered the conference room with his son-in-law in good spirits to give his final closing speech to the family members. In their mind's eye, the Rossos already saw themselves in the park of the villa in Palermo. Karl looked forward to having a good time at the pool with Marian and his wife could hardly wait to maltreat her beloved on the tennis court. The world seemed perfect, especially because absolute solidarity had prevailed amongst the members at the party on Saturday. But new problems were to arise in the upcoming meeting of which neither Karl nor his father-in-law had any idea about.

"Good morning everyone. Again I would like again to thank you heartily for the good work that each of you has accomplished here in the last few days. Yesterday crowned it all as I also was able to see your wives and children. You really gave me extraordinary pleasure. And for that my sincere thanks to all of you."

The audience stood up from their seats and applauded. As the applause trailed off, Michele called out: "Don Rosso, on behalf of us all I also would like to express our very special thanks for the meeting, the discussions that we had and the wonderful party."
Don Rosso had just intended declaring the meeting to be closed when Michele continued with his speech. Only now could you could recognize the true reason behind his special efforts regarding the changeover of

the organization. He hadn't used the secret meeting to describe the benefits of a return by the Mafia into the legitimate world. Rather, a further agreement had arisen from the meeting that had taken place without the Rossos. Now, wise Michele wanted to play his trump, he was simply waiting for the right time.

"Now, dear Don Rosso, we still have one concern," Michele began. "We would, however, prefer to discuss this with you within the old familiar community. Therefore, it's necessary that your son-in-law leaves the room."

Karl and Don Rosso looked at each other completely taken aback and not understanding what was going on here. Heavy-hearted, Karl reacted quickly in order to avoid creating any more confusion and left the conference room voluntarily. His father-in-law watched him with a blank look on his face. He was unprepared and didn't know how to respond to Michele's statement, nor did he know what this was all leading to.

After Karl had left closing the doors behind him, Michele continued: "I'll keep this short, dear Don, we are of the opinion that old traditions should not be violated, not even for security reasons. You simply brought a stranger to the meeting of the first rank, and then you present him to us as your successor. It has been a tradition for generations that the first rank can only be achieved through inheritance. We, and I mean all of us here, believe that this should not change in the future."

The cat was now out of the bag. Don Rosso looked

228

around, almost everybody showed their agreement with Michele's statement by nodding. The Don screwed up his face angrily and distinct frown lines could be seen on his forehead.

After arranging his thoughts he began: "So here lies the nub of the problem. The traditions. Well, for one, our fathers thought this through well, but now we have a different situation. We are reorienting ourselves and moving away from criminal business dealing to purely legitimate business. Now we need a person to learn this business from who has a lot of experience. Let's be honest, no one in this room has such knowledge. Karl has worked for half of his life as a department manager at a bank. Therefore, he knows this better than any of us."

Michele replied: "That may be so. Nevertheless, we are of the opinion that one of us should be your successor." Again, there was agreement in the room.

Suddenly Don Rosso opened his eyes wide, suddenly raised both arms to his chest and at the same time collapsed on the floor.
The audience jumped up from their chairs and ran to their boss who was writhing in pain on the floor. "Quick", shouted Michele, "call an ambulance, quick! Damn it!" And he tore Don Rosso's shirt open.

Antonio dialed the number of the hotel reception and shouted, "We need an ambulance straight away, in the conference room. Heart attack, probably! Hurry it up!"

The hotel reception called a doctor and alerted the ambulance. A few seconds passed before someone opened the door to the conference room and Karl called out: " Karl! Fast! Your father-in-law."

Karl hurried into the room and saw everybody standing helplessly around his father-in-law. He rushed to him, knelt before him and felt his pulse that was barely perceptible. The breaths were weak and irregular. He immediately started first aid activities giving mouth-to-mouth resuscitation. Then he heard a voice: "Please, let me through, I'm a paramedic." The paramedic was followed quickly by two more hotel employees who had a stretcher on wheels on which a breathing apparatus and an oxygen bottle were attached. The paramedic put the respiratory mask on Don Rosso, then he was lifted onto the stretcher. Then they raced to the elevator heading towards the first aid room on the ground floor to wait for the ambulance. Karl ran after them and those who remained in the room looked at each other helplessly and worried. None of them dared to say a word.
By the time the paramedic reached the first aid room with Don Rosso and the accompanying persons, the ambulance had already arrived.

They took a few quick examinations and said: "Suspected stroke, we need to take him to hospital immediately. Are you a family member?"

Karl replied: "Yes, I'm his son-in-law and I'll accompany him to the hospital."

The ambulance arrived with sirens and flashing

lights. Don Rosso was pushed into the emergency room of the hospital, and Karl was left alone. He immediately took his cell phone out of his pocket and called his wife". Marian, please stay calm, your father has just been brought to the emergency room of the university clinic with a suspected stroke."

"What," Marian cried desperately, "Dad is at the university clinic with a stroke! I'll be right there. She hurried to her limo and instructed the chauffeur quickly, "Take me straight to the emergency room of the university clinic, but quickly. "And the chauffeur immediately followed the order.

As soon as Karl had ended the call, one of the doctors came to him and said, "You can calm down a bit, Your father-in-law has not yet regained consciousness, but it's not as bad as we thought initially. He is now being well taken care of and was moved to the intensive care unit. It's good that you responded so quickly, Mr. Rosso."

Now one thing followed after another for Karl. Marian came running up to and cried, "Karl, what happened? How is my father doing? Where is he?"

"Calm down first of all, my dear," her husband tried to console her. "He is being well taken care of, I just talked to the doctor. After receiving first aid, your father has now been moved to the intensive care unit. But it doesn't look as bad as it did at the beginning. We can't do anything at the moment, he is still unconscious. Come on, let's go to the cafeteria and get some coffee."

Marian asked, "Karl, what happened? My God, I got such a fright."

Karl replied: "I don't know what happened, I was out of the room when it happened. Maybe the last few days and weeks have been too much for him."

Now his wife was unfair to him, "You should have been more careful. You know that he is no longer young. I have always preached to him that he should not work so much. Now look what happened."

They had just arrived at where the coffee was served in the hospital cafeteria and Karl ordered two coffees without defending himself from his wife. Marian was upset and close to tears. Her husband took her hand to calm her down.

"I'll stay here with my father," Marian said. "You can go back to the hotel and take care of everything You can come back again later. I'm going to the intensive care unit."

Karl drove back to the hotel without argument. There he was awaited eagerly by the members of the first rank who were waiting to get news about their boss. Karl willingly told them what the doctor in the hospital had said, adding that Don Rosso would probably be absent for a few days.

Michele said: "Close the door, we still have something to discuss. Karl, you may stay."

He added: "Given the situation, I will take over Don Rosso's chair in the interim or is there someone who doesn't agree? If so, please raise your hands." Nobody did therefore Michele was now the interim boss. Some of them glanced around questioningly. What would happen now?

"We continue as before. Up until the time when we know exactly how the Don is progressing. Tomorrow all of you can go home again. We will now end the conference and Karl can let us know how the boss is doing," Michele stated.

Karl listened intently and tried to make sense of the whole situation. He still did not know why the members had sent him out of the meeting, but he wanted to stifle his curiosity and not ask why. Karl noticed immediately that Michele wanted to take advantage of the situation and seize power. A bit later, when everybody had said their goodbyes and expressed their sympathy to Karl, they left the hotel.

Karl took a quick shower and returned to the clinic.

In the intensive care unit Marian sat at her father's bed looking very worried. Shortly before Karl had arrived, she had spoken with the attending doctor. Now she informed her husband that her father was out of danger and amazingly stable. As a precaution they had put him into an induced coma to make his body relax. Countless tubes and devices tended to his inanimate body. The doctor said it could probably take two to three days until the patient regained consciousness again.

"Karl, it's so good that you are here with me." Marian

looked at him sadly and they both sat helplessly at Don Rosso's bedside.

A few hours had gone by when Karl said softly, "Honey, let's go back to the hotel and get some sleep, the day was long enough. We can do nothing at the moment anyway and if anything new happens we will be notified immediately."

Marian replied: "No, Karl, I would rather wait here at his bedside until he wakes up. You can go back, it's enough that I stay here."

Karl was not really in agreement with that but in spite of all the persuasion, she wasn't to be dissuaded. Therefore, he reluctantly left her on her own in the hospital and was driven back to his hotel. In the suite, he put his pajamas on and quickly fell into a deep and dreamless sleep.

The next morning Karl awoke alone in his bed and needed a moment until he could think clearly again. He quickly jumped out of bed and went into the bathroom to get ready quickly. Then after eating a bread roll and drinking a cup of coffee he hurried back to the clinic. There was his wife with black shadows under her eyes after sitting at her father's bedside the whole night. She told him that her father had not made a single sound the whole night. Feeling helpless, Karl handed her the coffee that he had brought with him.

"You go back to the hotel and try and get some sleep," suggested Karl to his beloved Marian: "I will take over. Don't worry, if anything happens, I'll call you immediately, I promise."

Marian realized that she also needed to get a few hours sleep, and had herself driven back to the hotel.

Now Karl sat down beside the bed of the great Don Rosso and saw him lying there peacefully. He actually looked as he always did. His face even had its normal color again. An hour later, the doctors came to see the patient, muttering various Latin expressions. Then they left the hospital room and Karl followed them. He asked the senior physician about his father-in-law's condition. He told him astonished, "Mr. Rosso, your father-in-law is puzzling us. Although je is still in an artificial coma, his body functions all correspond to those of an able-bodied man. The examinations have yielded only positive results. We have no explanation for it, but he is in perfect health."

On the one hand Karl was very pleased with this statement, on the other hand, he doubted the results. Maybe the doctors had overlooked something? There had to be a reason for Don Rosso's sudden stroke.

He sat down again next to his father-in-law and waited.

It was not until late in the evening that his cell phone rang and Marian spoke at the other end of the line: "Hello my darling, I have just woken up, is there anything new?"

Karl calmed her down: "Nothing has changed. Your

father is well. The doctors are completely puzzled by his good condition. Have you eaten anything?"

Marian replied: "No, not yet, I think you should come back to the hotel, we will eat together and then I will go back for the night watch."
Karl agreed with this proposal and left the hospital.

Karl and Marian were sitting in the hotel restaurant for dinner when he asked her, "Has your father ever felt faint?"

She replied, "Never, he is examined regularly twice a year by his doctor who always confirmed he was in perfect health. But at his age unexpected things can sometimes happen. I am still very frightened. Maybe we should have my father's personal physician fly here as a precaution? What do you think?"

"Not a bad idea," Karl said. "It's always better to be safe than sorry. There must be a cause for your father's sudden collapse. I suggest we share the night watch, I will come and relieve you at about 2 o'clock. Beforehand, I will organize his doctor's flight from Palermo."

After dinner, the couple separated. Karl went back to the suite and made a call to the villa so the butler could inform the personal physician. He then ordered the private jet to Palermo to pick the doctor up. Marian took over the night watch at her father's bedside. He was still sleeping deeply.

At about 2.00 a.m. the hotel phone rang next to Karl's

bed. He woke up immediately and picked up the telephone receiver. A female voice answered: "Good
morning Mr. Rosso, it is 2,00 a.m., your wake-up call,
I hope you slept well."

"Yes, thank you very much," he replied, still in a daze
and got dressed. Then he went to the hospital to relieve the bleary-eyed Marian at the patient's bedside.
Nothing was different to the night before.

At dawn, just as Karl had just dozed off a little, he
suddenly heard a loud moan coming from his father-
in-law. Don Rosso rolled over in bed and wailed. "Oh,
my head".

Karl quickly pressed the emergency button. A nurse
and a doctor rushed immediately to the patient. They
calmed Karl down saying Don Rosso was now obviously slowly waking up from the artificial coma
which could only mean something good. It took several hours for him to wake up properly and Karl was
waiting by his side sleepily. Again and again, his father-in-law rolled over in bed with a loud moan.
When he finally regained consciousness and still completely dazed from the medication he asked, "Where
am I? Oh, Karl, are you here? Give me some water
please. What happened?"

Karl was overjoyed and poured him some water in a
glass letting him drink slowly. Gradually, Don
Rosso's head cleared and his son-in-law told him
what had happened. So that he didn't wake her up,
Karl sent Marian a text message saying that her father
had woken up and that he definitely felt better.

The doctors examined Don Rosso and were very surprised at how quickly he had recovered.

The doctors spoke of a miracle. Slowly, Don Rosso's memory came back. He said quietly, "Karl, close the door, I need to talk to you."

The supremo takes the throne away from the lobbyist

His son-in-law closed the door and Don Rosso contin-ued, "My memory has now fully returned. I now have a confession to make, but this must remain between you and me. I only felt faint for a brief moment in the conference room, but I used that opportunity to bring the meeting to an end. Because they didn't want to recognize you as my successor. Do you understand?"

Now Karl couldn't believe his ears. His father-in-law had faked everything? Everything was just a show? Karl felt violent anger build up inside him because Don Rosso had scared everybody to death. With his game, he had caused his daughter and others grief and sorrow for days and nights. Enraged and without saying a word Karl ran out of the room to the lavatory in order to cool his face with water. He could hardly believe that he had been deceived by his father-in-law in such a way. For him, Don Rosso's motivations and the fears that he had caused his family were totally unrelated.

Karl walked slowly back to the hospital room, opened the door and looked into the beaming face of the Don. Now Karl thought about how he should inform his frightened wife about this. Could he conceal this spec-tacle from her as his father-in-law wanted him to?
"We have to have a serious talk," Karl turned to his father-in-law. His anger made him brave. Don Rosso replied, "But you have to understand, I wasn't up to the situation because I was unprepared for it. Michele

tried to seize power behind my back. He is wise enough, as you could see. He immediately took advantage of the situation." "But now he has already reached his goal," Karl said. "In your absence he declared himself as interim boss on the throne. I was present, but there was nothing I could say. You have to take up your position again as soon as possible before something worse happens."

Together they decided that the boss should stay one more day in hospital to recover and then go back to Palermo with the couple and regain power. There was nothing for the son-in-law to do but hide the truth from his wife. However, to not leave his beloved Marian worried any longer he called the hotel to tell her that her father had recovered miraculously. When Marian heard this she couldn't stay in the hotel anymore and raced over to the hospital. Overcome with joy, she fell into the arms of the two men.

"Daddy, you're a bear, but a sweet one," she said to Don Rosso "you have to promise me to work more slowly in the future." Marian's father winked unnoticed at his son-in-law.

The following day Serjo Rosso was released from the hospital. The Rossos drove together to the hotel and prepared for their return flight to Palermo the next day. The personal physician who had already arrived in the meantime examined the boss and confirmed his perfect health. They arrived happily back at the villa. As always, the welcoming committee made up of domestic staff was waiting for them at the entrance. All three Rossos took a deep breath calling out almost all at the same time "Home at last!"

After a few hours of rest Marian began: "Karl, we haven't played tennis for such a long time. Maybe you have lost your skills already?" Karl parried: "Maybe, but tomorrow is early enough to refresh them." Marian pulled him over to the tennis court shouting: "Don't argue, you need some exercise. You rested enough during the last few weeks. You are not sick like my father." Karl had no chance to escape his wife and resigned himself to his fate. Meanwhile, Don Rosso was enjoying getting special attention and pity from everyone.

Nevertheless, the two Rosso men were drawn back to work the next day. The boss wanted to seize power back into his own hands straight away. "Today we will send a circular letter to all the members of the first rank," he said to Karl, and began to draft it:

"Dear friends, I have completely recovered and have taken up business activities again fully. I thank Michele for taking over leadership in the meantime, however I will continue again without restrictions. I will soon begin with the realignment process. I am very sorry that I couldn't say goodbye to you personally. We will see each other again at next year's meeting With best regards."

With a callous smile on his lips, he said to Karl: "Please encrypt it and send it to everybody including Michele. That will serve him as a lesson, I know how to assert myself in this matter." Karl followed his orders and went to work. He then asked the boss: "Tell me, do you mean that it's all already been decided? I mean, the fact that I am to be your successor. The Don replied, "It'll work out, I am quite sure of that. Moreover, they can't hold a candle to you anyway. After we have reorganized the business, they won't be able to have a say anymore anyway. We are not just talking about cashing in some protection money or selling a couple of packages of drugs, we are talking about tough business dealings in industrial companies. Don't worry, I'll handle it." Without leaving an opportunity for Karl to ask any further questions, Don Rosso made his way to the pool to read a newspaper. He was obviously again very pleased with himself and the world.

Karl and Marian also spent the rest of the day at the pool and returned to the villa again in blissful serenity. This wasn't even affected by the responses that arrived from the first rank members. They congratulated Don Rosso on his recovery with the kindest of words. Even Michele wrote a very conciliatory message in which you could read between the lines that he regretted his attempt to seize power. Don Rosso read the member's letters with relish and then jumped up and shouted to Karl: "You see, now they all got nervous. This will teach them a lesson. Nobody will try to take over my throne again."

Karl was working extremely hard on entering the information that he had received from the trustees on new company investments into his computer. A lot had accumulated again during his absence. He wrote a letter to his fellow board members at La Finette in Paris briefly explaining about the alleged meeting in

Dusseldorf and telling them that they had only discussed future company investments. His father-in-law was extremely satisfied.

Michele wasn't particularly pleased about the letter in which Don Rosso had informed him about his speedy return. Uncertain about his position, he asked the Don for a personal meeting at the villa as he felt fear and remorse. When Don read this, he laughed out loudly and told Karl about it. "Let him come and I'll show him where to go. He won't find me unprepared this time. And once and for all I can clear up the question of my successor. Send him a message that I expect him here in one week's time. He will experience a nasty surprise." Karl replied: "But do you really mean that? Is it not a little early? Should not we wait a bit until the furor has died down? Not that an argument develops and it all starts off again from the beginning."

"You have to fight," said the boss, "I can't let him intimidate me. Also, we have no time for such infantile games. We will need all the forces we have to establish a solid plan for the reorganization. This will not be an easy thing, I'm sure."

In the afternoon, Karl, laying on a lounger by the pool again thought about his past and the events of the last few years and months. He remembered how it had all started on the park bench at the Rhine and how he, after his promotion at the bank, became director of the company in Paris. Then they had an international meeting of the Mafia bosses. Everything had happened so fast that he had difficulty processing it.And the future was anything but certain.

Would he really be Don Rosso's successor in the future?

Would the Don be able to keep his family members at bay?

Were the bosses really prepared to support the long-term changeover of the Mafia that would take until the year 2020?

Could everything be implemented without harming the parties involved?

Could the criminal activities really come to an end? Questions upon questions opened to which he had no answer at this point in time. It will all continue in the next episode.